Forget-me-not Forever

Vanessa Åsell Tsuruga

About the author

Vanessa Åsell Tsuruga was inspired to write her first book *Forget-me-not Forever* by the friends for life that she made learning, living, and working all around the world. Raised in Sweden, Vanessa moved to Barcelona when she was thirteen. After graduating from an international school in 1997, she studied journalism in London with a gap year in Tokyo. She spent a few years in Kobe. Vanessa received her Master's Degree in Olympic Studies in Olympia, Greece. She lives in Tokyo with her husband and three children.

A letter from the author

September 26, 2020
Tokyo

Hello!

My grandmother gave me a journal for Christmas in 1989. I was eleven, and from that evening onwards, I wrote for twenty-one years without missing a day. I have recently picked it up again, and oh, it feels so good. Journaling has always been a way for me to channel everything that's going on in my head.

Ever since I was a child, I've loved writing letters. I had pen pals in many different countries and so curious to connect with people I had never met.

I enjoyed an idyllic childhood in Sweden. At thirteen, I moved to Barcelona when my father got a job there. I attended an international school and my circle of friends — which had always been solid — expanded into all corners of the world. I moved on to London, Tokyo, Kobe, back to Stockholm, Olympia, back to Kobe and then to Tokyo again — always staying in touch with friends through letters and postcards.

The words and the stories we keep telling ourselves and each other are what will keep us all connected. Letters, journaling, and friendship inspired me to write Forget-me-not Forever. I hope you will enjoy it.

I would love to hear from you, and I promise to write back!

Take care,
With love from Vanessa

Copyright

In memoriam

Hugo Nordmark

2008 — 2020

Dedication

A world of friendship — and where it all began…

Chris Wirszyla: Clam Power.
David Magaña: A sense of place. And the wonder of it all.

The world sisterhood.

The sister cities of Barcelona and Kobe.

Omnia mea mecum porto

All that is mine I carry with me

Stockholm, Sweden

April 2008

It was a Tuesday with a scent of coffee. I was more tired than usual, exhausted and completely without energy. The invitations lay in a big pile on the kitchen table. We'd been up all night stuffing and addressing envelopes. Our fingertips were colored gold from stamping *Wedding* in the upper corners. A morning kiss, with a glass of water in my hand, was the last thing we did. You had to go to a meeting, and I was left standing there, alone in my nightgown, looking at the pile of sealed envelopes. The words we had said to each other still hung in the air.

"You'll mail the invitations, right?" you had asked.

And my answer, "Of course, I'll do it."

Looking at the pile again — our wedding invitations, most with airmail stickers to the left of the stamps — I became dizzy. When the room finally stopped spinning, everything was suddenly crystal clear. It was like a still photo spliced into a movie. It lingered, longer than necessary, and any people watching in the theater would have started to squirm. Pause, push the button with two fat lines.

The cross-breeze of a thought flickered by, and the movie started to play again. The idea had visited me countless times before, but today it was like a straight shot to my heart. It was both a relief and incredibly painful. I immediately understood that it was now or never. And never didn't exist. I lost by knockout. No more rounds. Twelve years had gone by. I had to call and tell it like it was.

The fingers dialed numbers without thought. Thankfully, it went straight to voicemail. I took a deep breath and left a short and concise message. Not a lot of words, and "goodbye" was the last one. I packed some clothes and filled up a water bottle. Neither took very long. Then I made the other call.

Before I stepped out of our apartment, I left a note in the middle of the dinner table, held down by the stone we'd saved from our first date. *Don't forget to water the wedding bouquet. I planted the seeds in the flower box on the balcony. Kisses.* I had added in pencil, *I will always love you.* I'd hesitated, and almost, but didn't write, *independent of what happens.*

I took a big step over the doormat. Maybe it was out of respect for the goodbye kiss we'd shared over it, with me standing on my toes, less than half an hour before. I glanced at the garbage chute on the landing, with its ugly sticker always reminding people to tie their trash bags closed. I locked the door, turning the key with my backpack hanging over my shoulder and the invitations in my right hand. A selection of people chosen from the heart — family, relatives, and friends like Rosana, Selma, Mrs. Hewson, Yuzuki, and Clara Santos.

I took a taxi to Stockholm Central Station. It was the 26th of April 2008, and a long journey had just begun. Or one had just finished. Or it was a continuation that would keep going on and on.

My biggest regret was that our last kiss had tasted like stamps.

Paris, France

I put the pencil aside with the diary my mom had given me for my tenth birthday. I was born on January 14th, which is the Swedish name day for Felicia — my name. My mother always said that it was the happiest day of her life and that was exactly what my name meant: Joy, happiness. She'd bought the diary in Istanbul. It wasn't that big and not very thick. It felt like a friend I could always trust.

I looked again at the letter with the Swedish stamp of a sailboat, postmarked September 5th, 1988. I thought about what it would be like to sail on the seven seas, like letters that didn't go by airmail. On the back, Alma had written her return address above a sticker. It was a purple heart.

Hi Felicia!

How's Paris? I'm ten now too! Mom and Dad took me to the Gröna Lund amusement park, and then we spent the night in Stockholm before going back home. We stayed at the apartment of my mom's friend, who was away traveling. We had her whole place to ourselves, with a view of the cruise ships sailing out to Finland.

When can you and I go traveling like we always wanted to?

I slept in a bunk bed and looked out the window until I fell asleep, and I thought of you! I just wish we could live closer to each other.

I have great news about our secret project… Amelia. We got a letter in Spanish! I asked my mom to make a photocopy at her office. Read it after you finish this! I learned something new in Spanish: Amigas para siempre. Friends forever.

And another thing, I found a pretty tin box at a garage sale to keep the letters in.

Hugs and kisses from Alma.

PS I miss you more than you can imagine! Come home soon! Promise, please, thank you. Hugs from your friend forever.

I unfolded the copy of the handwritten letter from Clara Santos that had been neatly folded twice. Alma's mom had done a great job photocopying it. I pinned the copy up on the wall so that I could see it every day sitting at my desk doing homework. Our first letter! Our secret project — Amelia — had produced mail.

Queridas Alma y Felicia… The first line I understood, *Dear Alma and Felicia.* But after that, it quickly got more complicated. I needed help. It was almost four o'clock, so I put on my shoes and ran down to the square behind our house, where Señora Pilar always walked her dogs in the afternoon before going to the grocery store. We had talked a lot since I'd moved to Paris, and I loved her dogs. She knew that I went to the international school and that my mom worked at the embassy.

If I was lucky, Señora Pilar would be there soon. I brought my geography textbook to keep me occupied while I sat on a bench and waited. And waited. I had read the chapter on Lake Victoria three times and almost knew it by heart when the *Señora* approached the square with her three dogs. She lit up when she saw me. I took a good moment to pet the dogs, who jumped and happily nibbled at my pant leg.

"Felicia, *ça va?*"

"*Excusez-moi, pouvez-vous m'aider?*" I asked, having practiced a bunch of times how to politely ask for help.

We sat down on a bench under a plane tree. With the letter in her hand, Señora Pilar began translating to English.

Dear Alma and Felicia,

Thank you for inviting me into your secret club!

If only everyone continued to dream like when they were children! This is the first time that I'm writing a letter to someone I don't know. Still, it feels like we're already friends for life.

I have always admired Amelia Earhart. An iconic woman, someone we can literally look up to with all the solo journeys she took in the skies. You picked an excellent name for your binder. I have filled in my part and passed it on already. Amelia will make history!

I hope we can meet one day! Come and visit me in Cuba, and I will tell you my story. Until then, I send you my warmest wishes.

God bless you both.

Your friend,

Clara Santos.

I laid awake after my bedtime prayers that night, looking up at the dark ceiling. My imagination lept in an arch from my pillow in Paris to Santiago de Cuba.

* * *

Alma and I came up with our secret project — the binder — in the summer before fourth grade. We were trying to think of the smartest way to travel the world as ten-year-olds when I remembered Amelia Earhart. I'd done a school project about the American aviation pioneer.

"She flew solo across the Atlantic, and she also wrote a lot of books," I said.

"Maybe we can be like Amelia," Alma chimed in. "Let's create something that flies and picks up stories."

"Like a…?"

"…flying binder! Yes! A binder full of empty loose-leaf plastic sleeves that fill up as the journey continues."

* * *

The Summer Olympics were in Seoul that year. We sat glued to the TV, watching as Ben Johnson received and then had to give back his gold medal for the 100-meter sprint. Like many others, I was angry. How could he cheat?! I felt lied to.

Summer break ended, and I flew home to Paris. I started missing Alma before we even said goodbye. Summertime at our family lake house in the Hälsingland province, with the never-ending Swedish summer nights and my best friend as a neighbor, was the stuff of fairytales. I never wanted my time there to end.

The binder — Amelia — was quick off the starting blocks. In less than three months, it had traveled to Cuba, using different modes of transport along the way. It was our way to take a trip around the world since we were too young to go ourselves. Brimming with dreams, like all kids at that age, we wanted so much.

We had tried to build a submarine in Alma's dad's shed, but it hadn't worked. It took on too much water. We chased crows with homemade bows and arrows. We collected money for starving children in Ethiopia and ended up sending an envelope with four ten kronor bills and four single krona coins in it to Save the Children. We put up posters of Tom Cruise at the right height for kissing and wrote letters to politicians who wanted to close down the Inland Line, a railroad spanning more than a thousand kilometers in the north of Sweden. We baked bread and sold it in a stand on the sidewalk, started our own newspaper, and picked wildflowers to sell by the cemetery.

We were privileged, with the future in our hands and our dreams within reach. The binder was only known by us — and anyone who found it. Alma and I had even included top-secret letters, sealed and private from each other, for Amelia to guard.

Throughout the fall of 1988, more letters arrived from adventurers we had never met. Greetings from Alma always cheered me up, especially after a draining day at the international school I attended. One bright yellow letter lifted my spirits after a disappointing math test. The B+ I had received was light-years from the A- that I fought for. A careless mistake had messed things up.

Alma informed me in purple marker with a mix of uppercase and lowercase letters that another postcard had arrived from Yolanda Hewson in New York. Her late husband had served the United States foreign service his whole life, his last three posts as ambassador. Mrs. Hewson had settled back in Manhattan after decades living all over the world and went to the opera a few times a month, often with close friends. In her first letter, she'd enclosed a black-and-white photo of herself on a veranda with plants all around her. We guessed she was in her seventies.

Around Halloween, when my mom had decorated the outside of our front door with pumpkins, I sat down one evening with a cup of hot chocolate and my best ballpoint pen. It was the one that glided over the paper as if it were made of silk. I wrote on stationery I had received as a birthday gift from my neighbor and had saved for special occasions. I wrote a letter to Clara Santos in Santiago de Cuba and another to Mrs. Hewson in New York.

I wrote about how Alma and I had become friends the summer before first grade. We had met down by the water next to our family lake house in Hälsingland, just a few hours by car from Stockholm. I had been fishing, on my own, with a radio as my only company, and she had come by with a bowl of strawberries and said: "Hi, my name is Alma, what's your name?" We talked about Sweden and all the places I'd lived: Buenos Aires, Maputo, Stockholm, Beirut, and Paris.

I licked closed the airmail envelopes in thin paper with blue and red-leaning lines along the edge. From Paris, westward to America and Cuba. Envious of the movement awaiting the letter, I imagined transforming into a postcard, diving into the mailbox by the bakery, where I would be collected by the postman and sent away to the other side of the world.

Where was Amelia now? What destination was it headed to next?

A few hours before 1991 became 1992, Alma called and told me another letter had arrived. This time from Barcelona. Where the famous architect Antoni Gaudí's masterpieces lined the streets, including the La Sagrada Familia basilica with its steeples reaching up like fingers to the sky, their manicure of mosaics and ornaments glistening in the sun. It was a city getting ready to host the Olympic Games. Another letter flew in from the Land of the Rising Sun. We heard from people in Greece, Mongolia, Argentina.

Amelia was really moving around. Our world was growing.

Stockholm, Sweden

December 16, 1996

I arrived, eighteen years old and homeward bound for one of my many places to call "home sweet home." Newspapers jammed in the seatback pockets were filled with reports of cold and chilly weather. We were in for a tough winter.

Seat belts clicked through all the rows, and everyone wanted out, quickly and immediately. A fast-paced panic had broken out after just a couple of hours on the plane. No one was spared; everyone was instantly infected. *I cannot wait to get off this plane* echoed in the silence.

We'd barely made it off the plane before the refrains of passengers' cell phones turning on blended into a mobile phone version of the *Melodikrysset* musical game show. The typical *Absolute Arlanda* soundtrack followed us down the stairs. I eavesdropped on the chattering around me: the short descriptions of the supercool Christmas window displays and street decorations in London; the shopping at Harrods with afternoon tea at Fortnum & Mason, as well as a stroll through Hyde Park; and someone says they saw the Queen walking her corgis near Buckingham Palace, which sounded too good to be true and probably it wasn't. Suitcases rolled over the joints in the floor, their wheels clattered. There were questions about the meeting, the kids, and if dad was in the parking lot.

Teargas, a sign proclaimed above a white box on a pole. Swedish law didn't allow for teargas and pepper spray, so passengers were encouraged to voluntarily leave any they had on them in the box to avoid penalty. I started humming "Tears in Heaven" and was overwhelmed for a second by a sharp sadness.

A fit lady wearing an official-looking blue vest and with calves like upside-down bowling pins flew by on a scooter. A man on the loudspeaker sounded friendly as he warned us about unattended bags. We navigated through passport control and were channeled like boats on the Göta Canal to the world outside. Its name was Sweden. "*Thou mountainous North,*" according to the national anthem. But unlike the last line of the song, I didn't want "*to live… to die in the North.*" I wanted to live life in the world.

Suitcases paraded around on carousels in the baggage claim area. There were mutterings from the travelers who had to wait longer than others. Someone was angry that they had to pay for the baggage carts. The air was filled with hurry and some tired anger. Everyone wanted to get out, get home, to work, to the computer, to the printer, to that meeting, and to the kids.

Baggage carts raced past the bathrooms; most left the building with nothing to declare. I got my bag before everyone else — a world-first for me. This trip was starting out great, and it seemed like it would only get better.

* * *

The sparks of joy that crackled in the thousandth of a second when our brown and blue eyes met could have ignited a *majbrasa* — the Walpurgis Night bonfire. Like the many times I had arrived at Arlanda airport before, I was greeted with a smile off the charts. A cry of joy beyond any musical notes. Happiness personified — dressed in a long winter coat and belcher that hung over her shoulders — with helium balloons and flowers. Tulips in December. I loved her. Alma. My friend Alma. A landmark individual, overflowing with smiles and compliments rising like a soufflé. She was the custodian of our friendship.

"Feliiiiiiiiiciaaaaaaaaaaaaaa!" she yelled while scrambling through the packs of baggage carts. She planted herself directly in the way of the hurrying people that were on their way out and hugged me the way only Alma could.

She had learned a few tricks of the trade from an American whose business card claimed he was a "Certified Hugging Instructor" from the "Ministry of Love & Affairs." He had been passing through Uppsala one summer, stopping to sell his "hug competence" at Vaksala Square for fifty Swedish kronor. On her way home from a cousin's graduation party, Alma had negotiated the price down to a cup of coffee. Affection had flared between them — starting with a big, unforgettable hug and finishing in the exact same way on a train platform three hours later — when he had to continue heading north to Umeå. That cup of coffee had been an exceptionally lovely investment.

All the bits of happiness inside of me grabbed hold of each other and started moving around. They did the

Swedish *hambo* folk dance, the salsa, and then the jitterbug throughout all my limbs. Tears pinched in the corner of my eye, coming out shyly but firmly. The more reserved in the crowd fully ignored us. Others peeked, hiding their tears by pretending to adjust their glasses or rubbing the corner of their eyes. A red-haired woman in a bright yellow coat openly sought eye contact with me and smiled. She held the leashes to two dalmatians with big bow ties around their necks. They were sitting calmly, but as soon as they sensed love in the air, they jumped up and frantically waved their tails. Smiles as light as butterflies spread across the airport vestibule.

Our higgledy-piggledy greeting and gushing Q&A continued all the way out to the parking lot. Alma explained that she didn't have cash for the parking fee and had instead left a note begging any potential attendant not to give her a ticket, pleading that she was a poor student who had just gotten her driver's license. As soon as we saw her car, we knew it had worked. There was no ticket. The note was still there, but the bag of *Ahlgrens Bilar* car-shaped candies she'd left with it was gone.

"Yes," yelled Alma. "Say yes to yes!"

Our stomachs ached from laughing as we struggled to fit my bags into Alma's compact Volkswagen Golf. It hadn't occurred to her to leave the guitar at home, as well as the crate of empty bottles for recycling, and a box of puzzles that were now too childish for her little siblings, twins Hugo and Eulalia. An elderly couple, who parked in the space next to us, paused on their way in to check on our progress. They couldn't resist Alma's charms and promised to donate the puzzles to the church, where the lady volunteered once a month.

The angry wind of Arlanda hit me in the face. I breathed in the sharp snowflakes that swirled in the cold air and tickled inside my warm nose before disappearing forever. Chilly clouds billowed with each exhalation. My friendship with Alma had kept a constant, low burning flame in my heart that raised in intensity as soon as I was in her presence. We became one from the get-go. No pause, no awkwardness, no hassle. Alma seemed to carry in her a filing cabinet where she saved and sorted things like my teachers' names or what I got up to on any given Sunday. She knew what I ate for breakfast, how I got to school, and what I learned in history class. Her ability to be ever-present while absent was Alma's greatest gift.

Every time I came here, I marveled at this country. I took in the road markings, cars keeping the speed limit, and even a taxi driving by. Swedish advertising, Swedish scenery, Swedish Sweden. I was a stranger visiting my home. For me, the Swedish saying "Away good, at home the best" was more like "At home good, but away the most." I always felt a sense of satisfaction whenever I glimpsed the BBC's global weather map and managed to know a person in a specific place that was highlighted and would almost shout a "Yes!" if I could think of someone I knew in every city mentioned in the span of one report. A world of friendship — that's just how it was — from attending preschools and schools in Buenos Aires, Maputo, Stockholm, Beirut, Paris, and London.

What the national anthem called *"the quiet, thou joyful [and] fair"* swept by outside the car. Discounted Levi's jeans and thousands of parking spaces tempted drivers to roadside shopping centers. Sweden. Gas stations with *Kexchoklad* chocolate bars and porn on the top shelf, along with the *Absolute Music* pop compilation CDs and VHS videos to rent. *Varm korv*, which literally meant "warm sausages," but were just hot dogs. A ton of candy. JC Jeans on billboards and GB ice cream, which got a bit more expensive each year. Why did they have to raise prices all the time? My country, *"thou greeted me, loveliest."*

"It's so awesome that you're here," Alma chirped. "And in the winter! My building's co-op association bought some kicksleds that we can use!"

I felt a spark of recognition. Kicksleds — no doubt the most entertaining means of winter transport ever — were pretty much chairs mounted on skis. As kids, we always tried to go faster and faster on the hills next to the lake house. Alma would be sitting down, and I would be standing behind her, holding the wooden handlebars tight, propelling us firmly forward with one foot, the other kicking backward on the ground.

Heading back from the airport to Alma's house, our positions were reversed. Alma was driving and I was the passenger, wrapped in a doughy picnic blanket with pine needles stuck to the fabric. Headlights shone through the windshield wipers' arch every time we crossed paths with another car. I noticed the Swedish license plates. Three letters, three digits. Some cars had an *S* sticker. I was in

Sweden alright. Nothing was as familiar as those three letters and three numbers.

This would be my first Christmas in Sweden as an adult — my parents and I hadn't been back for the holidays in many, many years. The world was so big with so many places to choose from. My parents had visited more than sixty countries together since they'd shared a table at a café in Lima, Peru. They were both twenty-three. My mom had just started her career in the foreign service and my dad was already well into his life of academic pursuits. It was easy for him to join her on postings, working as a research fellow at universities in Washington, D.C., New Delhi, Casablanca, and Buenos Aires. That's where I came into the picture: in Argentina. It's no wonder I loved tango so much; my mother danced when she had me in her belly.

Every year around the middle of October, we — Mom, Dad, and I — would sit down to debate where to spend Christmas. We'd each have to come up with a potential location and make our case to the others. Then, we would each score all the destinations on a scale of one, two, or three points.

Our family lake house in the Hälsingland province was the undisputed winner 1996 with a full count of nine points, well above both Dublin and Vienna. My dad's illustrious description of the "Viennese Waltz" hadn't convinced me, and Dublin was just too close to our current home in London. A few days later, Dad went out to his favorite bookstores across town — a ritual for any upcoming family trip. He came home with the tote bag full of recommendations from his book-loving friends. There, and in the company of books, our journey always began, going through words on sometimes yellowed pages in novels, guidebooks, and biographies.

It had me wonder about how many books there were in the entire world. If you could know that number and how many words they contained, like a world word count. And if you could know that, then couldn't you distill it all into a single, simple sentence? Could that one sentence capture the meaning and point of it all, of life? Was that possible? Could you, without knowing all the books and words in the world, still write it? That life sentence?

* * *

On the plane to Stockholm, I had tried to describe in my journal the thoughts buzzing in my head. It was exciting to be on my way home, where we would have a Christmas celebration spiced with influences from all the places we had lived over the years. A mosaic of world customs. The year was almost over, and Alma had been a source of joy for me all through it. Phone calls with spring updates about the bird nest on her balcony, thick letters with pressed autumn leaves, and plenty of the vintage postcards she always bought blank at garage sales and filled with her updates. Her little, big gestures made thousands of kilometers feel like measly millimeters. What a luxury it would be to bask in each other's presence for several days in a row while I stayed in her apartment.

"When will you head up north?" I asked.

"I have to write a paper that's due in January, so I'll head up the day before Christmas Eve. And you?"

"I'm taking the train to Bollnäs on the 20th. We have a full four days together!"

Alma overtook a BMW and asked when my parents would be joining me at the lake house.

"They land on the 22nd and rent a car at Arlanda. Mom asked me to start getting the Christmas decorations out. I can't wait for our families to hang out together, just like the good old days!"

Even though Alma and I had hardly lived in the same country, a decade of friendship had glued us together. We were now eighteen years old and would soon get our first yearly orange letters from the Swedish Pensions Agency.

In about half a year, we would both graduate from high school. Alma would finish her studies at the Marina Läroverket — an independent high school that incorporated sailing and an oceanic atmosphere — in the Stockholm suburb of Stocksund. Meanwhile, my twelve years of schooling were set to be capped off with an international baccalaureate degree from the International School of London. I would march alongside classmates from all over the world to the sound of "Pomp and Circumstance" while we wore the iconic cap and gown. I'd been chosen to give a speech — I was planning one about taking on the world just like Amelia Earhart — and after that, I'd receive my diploma. I'd move the tassel of my cap from the right side to the left and join my class in one exuberant and unforgettable cheer while throwing our hats in the air.

* * *

The cold from the street blasted us as soon as we opened the car doors when we got to Näsby Allé, a half-hour ride from Stockholm. We took deep breaths and braved the subzero temperatures as we hurried to enter the code to unlock the front door of Alma's building. Her apartment was on the third floor and had belonged to her grandmother Anna-Karin before she passed away a year earlier. Seventeen-year-old Alma had graciously accepted to move in, and it was a pretty sweet setup for everyone involved. The building was right next to the Roslagsbanan train line — providing a quick commute to Stockholm, with the stop for Alma's school on the way. The Lindgren family home on the Näsby Castle estate, where her parents and siblings lived, was right across the street.

The stairs were a light gray linoleum with confetti flakes in blue and yellow cascades. There was the aroma of mulled wine and a garbage chute. *Tie the trash bags closed*, a sign demanded. A welcome mat in front of the apartment door said, *Stay away if you're not nice.* A handwritten sign proclaimed *I get a hernia from carrying junk mail. Save the trees!*

Alma put the key in the lock and turned. A strip of sleigh bells hung from a red satin ribbon on the coat rack and jingled as we brushed against them while hanging our winter coats. The apartment smelled of Alma. I took off my shoes and put on a pair of slippers that she had set aside for me. They were from Bangladesh, and she had found them at

Stadsmissionen, a charity store close to Odenplan plaza in Stockholm.

In the foyer was a round carpet that I could tell had belonged to Alma's grandmother. Two tulips thrived inside a red vase I had bought for Alma in Ecuador. They leaned against the wall mirror, like teenagers putting on make-up together. Just like us, only a few years ago, and even today when we had the chance — although it wasn't as often as one would like these days.

Advent candles lit up the kitchen window on the left. Just about every house in Sweden had something similar this time of year. The electric candle-shaped lightbulbs in pyramid-shaped holders could be seen shining in countless windows as soon as it got dark in the early afternoon. A potted ivy on the windowsill meandered up towards the ceiling, over the window, and down the other side. A hyacinth, with that distinct scent of Christmas, sat atop a dining table with four mismatched chairs. The table looked like it was being used for a kindergarten art class. Scattered all over it in Christmas joy and glory were colored tissue paper — in pink, purple, red, blue, and green — scissors, stickers, stamps, embossed scrap reliefs with angel motifs, felt-tip pens, and envelopes.

On the other side of the hallway was the tiny bathroom that reminded me of the one on my flight that morning. My knees would almost hit the door when I closed it. The shower curtain print was the phrase *I am beautiful* repeated in different languages. A couple of toothbrushes leaned against each other, their bristles kissing, in a glass on the sink. On the shelf was a blue candle, just a little burnt out, and five miniature perfume bottles from a trip abroad.

Alma's bedroom was only wide enough to accommodate her bed and nothing else. It was a room just for sleep. "And love," she giggled. Wide silk fabrics hung from the ceiling in the living room, which had been turned into a lounge of pillows and cushions since my last visit. The TV had been replaced with a Kalaha board game on a low table.

"I want to turn this into a cozy game den," Alma said. "I'll invite friends over, and we'll all sit like hippies with our legs crossed, light some incense, and play Trivial Pursuit. How's that for a great time?"

I felt more at home here than anywhere else in the world. An unprecedented sense of belonging. The boundless dreams hovering in Alma's atmosphere made it so unique — there was no other place like this. There was a tangible desire to enjoy life to the fullest, contagious for those who dared to seize the moment before it was gone. *Carpe diem.* And it was always with her, and she was so bull's eye and spot-on in capturing it. She found quirky things to try and could make my stomach scream for more of her olives, homemade hummus, or sun-dried tomato spread. Alma was a sudden voice in the night or an unexpected postcard in the mailbox, always arriving so effortlessly.

* * *

It had been almost six months since we had last seen each other. We'd met up in London over the summer and gone on a cycling trip to Wales. So much had happened since then. Questions, lots of questions. Our dialogue traversed between verb forms, like a car weaving through traffic, between then, now, and later.

"So," I started, "guess what I thought about when the pilot gave the 'welcome onboard we will soon get going' spiel?"

"You thought about going to aviation school!" Alma threw out without any thought.

"Nope. Let me give you a hint. The pilot was a woman."

"I know now! You thought about Amelia."

"You got that right!"

"I wonder where our binder is. I have a feeling it's going to come back," Alma said confidently. "Even though it's been eight years and quite a while since it disappeared..."

"How far can we track Amelia?"

Alma walked over to a small cabinet by the window. She gently removed one of her grandmother's crocheted blankets that hung over the door, like the bangs on a first grader, opened it, and retrieved a tin box. It was the one she'd written about in the letter all those years ago that had cost her five Swedish kronor at the garage sale. It was painted a garish pink and adorned with small hexagonal mirrors framed in gold wire. A little Christmas joy. A piece of paper was stuck on the inside of the lid:

Bought in 1988. In this box, we will collect all our letters.

"In a way, I don't want to start digging into it," Alma said. "If Amelia comes back, Amelia comes back. *Que será, será.* It was smart of us to write my family's address on the back cover! Your family's all nomads, but mine's rooted across the road as firmly as an old pine."

"We did promise to reimburse every penny for postage," I said. "But it might be pricey, like DHL."

"Trust me," Alma said, attempting to sound reassuring, "whoever fills in the last plastic sleeve will send the binder home to Dad. Amelia will return, maybe she's already on her way?"

It was a common refrain between the two of us. If Alma cranked the window down in a hot car, I was the one who cranked it up and waited for the air conditioning to kick in. It was in my nature to be more guarded and downbeat, while Alma was carefree and hopeful. She was convinced that we would see the binder again. I was skeptical.

* * *

That night, I shared with Alma the thoughts that had been marinating in my mind for a while. She was the first person I told that I was considering taking a year off. I had one life; I should live it.

"Okay, let's make a deal," Alma said with that diplomatic look on her face, just like my ambassador mother. "We're both graduating this summer. School is out, and it's time to celebrate our achievement. Let's find everyone who knows about Amelia — everyone who joined our secret club. We'll just go."

I could feel the travel bug biting into me. It was probably the exact moment I crossed the point of no return. Something was starting to grow in me. But I was still cautious.

"Sure," I said sarcastically. "I'll just contact the universities I'm applying to and say 'Thanks, but no thanks.'"

"They'll all still want you, even if you start a year later! All of them will be shouting 'We want Felicia! We want Felicia!' with big placards about scholarships!"

It then hit me that I would be the first-ever in the Äng family to take a gap year! A pioneer. It would be scandalous. My path had been made clear early on: Do well at school, study at a fine university, and get a rewarding job at a government agency or institution in the capital with a name that sounded affluent and weighty, like the Ministry of Foreign Affairs or the Swedish Institute.

"They'll understand it all someday," Alma said as if she had read my thoughts, "but it may take a while."

Talking about the future with Alma was like standing at an open gable window and feeling a chill fall breeze on your face.

"Let's make a documentary about Amelia and sell it to the BBC!" I said with a laugh.

"No, seriously," Alma said. "Let's pinky swear right now that we're really going to travel," Alma said. "Nothing can get in our way. We'll go together."

Alma pulled out a stamp pad from the same cupboard where the tin box of letters had been stored. One by one, we pressed our pinky fingers so that the ink bubbled to the edges, then intensely rubbed them together for a long time, and each left a fingerprint on a blank Christmas card. Alma wrote her address on it. She asked me to go to the post office the next day and mail it.

"It's always fun to get a letter, even if you expect it!"

* * *

Good morning, Sweden. It was already ten o'clock when I got up from the mattress on the living room floor and read the note Alma had left for me.

> *Good morning, didn't want to wake you. I have to work a little bit on the paper that's due after Christmas. Help yourself to tea and sandwiches. I'll be back at four. Can't wait! Hugs until I'll see you! Yippie! A.*

I turned on the radio and listened to the black ice warnings from the Swedish Meteorological and Hydrological Institute. It had frosted over during the night and was getting even colder. The hospitals were overloaded with broken bones from slips and falls. The thermometer showed -13 °C and I could hear the faint sounds, out there in the cold, of the railroad crossing coming down as a train slowed and stopped at the Näsby Allé station outside the kitchen window. It was the soundtrack that played here every twenty minutes. The mail slot rattled from the postman's delivery. I found mailings from Save the Children, Amnesty International, and Greenpeace, along with a postcard from the Azores, and a letter from Germany, judging by the postmark.

The answering machine on the stool in the hallway was flashing red. I pushed play and heard the Northern accented voice of Alma's father, Bruno, saying that a delivery notice had just arrived… for both of us. I rushed to slip into my boots and put on my down jacket. As I ran down the stairs two steps at a time, the final words of Bruno's message popped in my mind: *"Felicia, it is icy out there. Please be careful."*

I found Bruno just across Djursholmsvägen, the road in front of Alma's apartment. He was unlocking his café in the old gatehouse on the road that led into Näsby Castle. I couldn't help greeting him with a heartfelt hug.

"Let's go inside and warm up," he said. "It's so good to see you! You look great!"

Bruno took over the space for his café when the previous owner — who had traded old coins and stamps — moved to a nearby home for Alzheimer patients. That was fifteen years ago. Bruno's photographs hung on the walls above four small tables, a sofa, and chairs with pillows in different designs from the Red Cross store in Näsbypark. The cold pressed in on us. Bruno moved the heater closer to my feet and brought a basket of blankets over. He wrapped one around my shoulders and handed me his portfolio. Flipping through his new photo series on the homeless in wintertime, I was seized immediately — and with no remorse — by the relentless cold piercing the woman on the first page.

"She didn't make it very long after this shot was taken," Bruno said, pausing for a moment. "It's on display at Grillska Huset in the Old Town, and a gallery in Frankfurt has shown some interest. Any proceeds go to the charity I set up a few years ago."

Bruno went into the kitchen. He seemed content. His café always embraced me, whispering in my ear that my dreams would soon be butterflies, ready to fly off. He returned with a *lussebulle,* saffron bun, on a small ceramic plate with holly decorations along the edge.

"I got you something for Christmas," he said and handed me a wrapped present. "Maybe I'm ruining the surprise, but it's a series of photographs titled *Belle Amie.*"

Bruno explained there's a ship named *Belle Amie* docked close to Marina Läroverket, Alma's high school. And what he said next would always stay with me, "You are beautiful friends for life. You are each other's port and always will be."

Belle for beautiful, *Amie* for friend. Alma was my *Belle Amie* and I was hers.

* * *

"Hi, one stamp, please," I said, sliding over the Christmas card with my pinky fingerprint next to Alma's. "Domestic."

The cashier read the address and gave me a questioning look.

"It's not going very far. I live in that neighborhood. It's just seven minutes away from here by foot. You don't want to save a few bucks and just walk it over? It'll be faster for sure, especially now with all the Christmas cards!"

I shook my head.

"No, thanks. I'd like a stamp, please. How long will it take before it arrives?"

"Usually just a couple of days, but with the holidays and the weather, you never know. Every time the postmen go out for their deliveries, we tell them to be extra careful. It's so damn slippery out there, excuse my language. We can't afford to lose anyone now. It'll be there by Christmas Eve if you're really lucky, but you never know. Are you sure you want to mail it?"

"Yes, I'm sure. I also have this delivery notice."

It took her a while to find the package. People in line who didn't have a minute to spare sighed impatiently. She took the hint and called "Cecilia to the cashier, Cecilia to the cashier, please," in the PA system, and soon returned with beads of sweat on her forehead.

"Thank you very much," I said, looking at the sender's address. Japan.

I could hardly contain my emotions. I ran down to the bookshop on the ground floor of Näsbypark Centrum and bought a travel journal and a copy of *Bonniers World Atlas*. I hurried back to Alma's apartment and probably shaved a couple of minutes off the average time it takes to walk along Djursholmsvägen road. My palms were sweaty, but not from the heat of my *Lovikkavante* mittens. I was so jittery it took me three tries to punch in the front door code correctly. My emotions were running off-road with the pedal to the floor.

I put the key in the lock and turned. The bells on the coat rack jangled as I hung my coat up. There was the smell of Alma and my slippers from Bangladesh waited for me at the door. Thirsty from the speedy walk, I poured a large glass of water and gulped it down before making space for the package on the kitchen table. I simply stared at it for several minutes. My thoughts were all over the place. I made some hot chocolate and cupped my hands around the mug as I ate twelve *pepparkakor* gingerbread cookies.

The blank spaces after *Belongs to:* on the first page of the new travel journal were soon filled out in black ink with *Alma Lindgren and Felicia Fanny Äng*. The blue hour of the sun just below the horizon invited me to an intimate moment before the darkness took hold. Any moment now, the sounds of a slowing train would hint my best friend would soon come through the door, out of breath from running up the stairs two steps at a time.

It was carbon black outside when Alma — red-cheeked from the cold — sat down next to me on the floor in the living room. A pot of Darjeeling tea with matching cups sat on a Christmas tray next to us.

"Guess what," I said. "Amelia is back."

The neighbors downstairs probably heard the thump of Alma's chin dropping to the floor.

* * *

We opened the padded parcel together. The postage stamps were images of small birds overlaid with Japanese calligraphy. Even with Christmas right around the corner, nothing could compare with the excited anticipation. It was like the prelude to a wedding night. The binder — Amelia! — lay wrapped in tissue paper decorated with small gold stars inside a light blue cloth bag.

We were fourth graders when we'd left the binder at Jontas Burgers, a roadside burger joint along Route 50, which cuts through Sweden's Hälsingland province. It was hard to fathom that it had come back. It was a bit tattered, like a hippie after hitchhiking through a rough winter. We opened the binder and saw my swinging writing style through the first transparent plastic sleeve.

Hello!

We are Alma and Felicia, and the binder you are holding in your hands is our secret project. Welcome! Join the club.

We don't know how you got the binder, or who gave it to you, but we think there is a reason why it's with you now. Time will tell!

This binder has a secret code name: Amelia. We read about Amelia Earhart in school. She was a pioneer who proved that women could fly! Just like her, we love adventure. We want to be like her, but we are just starting fourth grade, so we are letting Amelia do the flying for us.

We hope this binder — Amelia — will collect stories from all over the world.

There are thirty loose-leaf plastic sleeves in total. One is yours to fill.

1. *Flip to the first empty plastic sleeve.*

2. *Write your name and address on the label.*

3. *Enclose anything you want that fits inside the plastic sleeve.*

4. *Close the zip so that everything stays in place.*

5. *Pass the binder — Amelia — onto another adventurer.*

6. *If you fill out the last plastic sleeve, please send Amelia back to this address — we will pay you back for sure!*

Alma Lindgren & Felicia Fanny Äng

C / O Bruno Lindgren

Näsby Slott

Djursholmsvägen 30

SE-183 52 Täby

Sweden

We promise to contact everyone when the binder returns to us one day. Thanks for giving Amelia wings to fly across the world!

Bon voyage!

Sincerely,

Alma Lindgren and Felicia Fanny Äng

PS: Please write to us after you've passed Amelia on. We can be pen pals while we wait for the binder to come home!

We smiled at each other, still in disbelief. I translated the slightly simplified versions of the original text in Spanish, French, and Portuguese. I teared up as I realized how much Portuguese I had forgotten since we left Maputo.

"Feels like a U.N. meeting," Alma giggled. "But without the earpieces and the monotonous interpreters."

The second plastic sleeve held the two letters Alma and I had written to each other. *Open after I am dead* in solid red marker left no doubts about Alma's instructions. On the back, she had put a heart sticker underneath her name.

"Oh, that's a clear message," I laughed. "Thankfully, you're still alive, so I don't have to open it today!"

"I'm actually really dumb," Alma exclaimed. "What if you die before me?! Did I think you'd rise from the grave with a letter opener?…"

"Well, maybe I should just pack one when I go — just in case! Like the Egyptians, getting ready for the afterlife!"

We broke out in a round of laughter that put us both on the floor.

"So, what about your letter?" Alma asked when we finally calmed back down. "Should I read it?"

"You know what, just wait until the time is right!"

* * *

We were ten years old and enjoying our summer vacation when Bruno bought us lunch that day in 1988 at Jontas Burgers. Since then, thirty empty plastic sleeves had been filled with life stories. Our brains were in overdrive. It was way past midnight when we finally started planning our trip around the world. We were going to meet Amelia's co-pilots. The countdown had begun, and we'd leave after we were done with school.

That left us with six months to scrape together enough cash for the trip. It felt light years away from our winter darkness, pitch black outside, and -16 °C. But summer would come, as all summers do.

Hälsingland province, Sweden

Almost Christmas

Our family lake house in the country was located just outside the locality of Alfta. It had been in the family since way before I was born. Childhood memories had slowly but surely crafted the house as an image of pure happiness in my mind. It was somewhere where everything had its place. I came here in the summers. I'd swim in Voxnan River or nearby Lake Grängen, play with Alma, and stay up as late as I wanted to every night. That magic had somehow remained, despite all the changes that came from merely existing.

I had grown older. I had a mobile phone and a bank account. Pop groups had come and gone. Roxette, Madonna, R.E.M. My wardrobe had been emptied and refilled — cute summer dresses and sandals were put aside when grunge took over with Dr. Martens, black jeans, and print T-shirts. By now, my outfits were relatively low-key: mostly blue denim and monochrome cotton shirts.

The area around the lake house had changed as well. Like many other rural towns, independent stores run by local owners had been gobbled up by chain stores with expansive aisles of frozen meals and TV dinners. Gas stations that had coupled their businesses with car mechanics and a café for *fika* — coffee and pastries — gave self-service an honest attempt before shutting down forever.

But maybe that's how things went?

*** * ***

During all our years abroad, we had always made active efforts to dig deeply into the area we lived in. In Maputo, we explored every corner of Mozambique. My favorite Sundays from back then were spent heading to the unspoiled beaches on the Indian Ocean, where the local restaurants flourished. We bonded with the community. Lifelong friendships began at vegetable and fruit stands, talking to the owners whose goods — and stories — were woven into our lives. Weekend trips to the markets became rituals. After we moved on, we stayed in touch, receiving pictures of newborn grandchildren named after other friends we'd brought along to the markets and introduced.

Maybe that's why my family loved Knåda Sport. A short car ride from the lake house, it was a local gem. Every summer, we would pop in to buy new shoes, badminton rackets, and bicycle parts — as well as catch up with the owners on what was going on in the area. If they were available, we would also stock up on whatever we could get in a size larger. It gave me room to grow. The rhythm of giving and receiving was steady in our lives. We would donate the shoes and clothes that I grew out of to a local charity wherever we were living.

I loved coming to Hälsingland. The lake house, with its painted white wood siding, lay between the defunct railway tracks and the fields that extended right down to the Voxnan River. The house, and surrounding property, was where my grandmother had grown up and it was a constant in my life. We owned it. It was ours — unlike our homes in Buenos Aires, Maputo, Stockholm, Beirut, Paris, and London, where we were just tenants passing through. Pulling up to the driveway always shot a sense of belonging straight into my heart.

Grandma's decorative copper pot had its place and my bathrobe had its place. The stone in the creek had its place. The air scented with lily of the valley, the view over the lake, and the birch tree next to the fence; all had their place. Everything that grew here had grown bigger but always with the same roots. The wallpaper was still the original; we hadn't changed it. Pine trees on the property had grown taller, and some had overturned in winter storms. The fabric along the seat of the kitchen nook bench was worn down from all the kids' legs over the years. There was a sense of place.

* * *

One by one, I carried the boxes of Christmas decorations from the attic down the steep stairs. All that was missing was a Christmas tree. I slipped my feet into a pair of boots a couple sizes too big. But doubling up with an extra pair of thick socks did the trick and they were less wobbly. Plus, the extra socks helped against the -15 °C chill outside. I walked over to our neighbor Stefan, to make sure if his offer to cut down a tree on his land for us was still good.

"As long as I live, and even when I'm in the grave, you're welcome to a Christmas tree every year. You have my word on that," he said when he saw me, and then smiled a typical Stefan smile.

We drank *Julmust* Christmas soda, ate *lussebullar*, and talked about the years that had passed since I last spent a winter in Hälsingland. When we finally made it to the woods, the trees were silhouetted against the darkening sky — still a shade of cobalt blue before going black — and all looked identical. I picked a tree at random, Stefan handed me the saw, and I cut it close to the ground. When it was free, he grabbed the tree at the bottom, and he led our two-person operation back to our house. After Stefan left, I took a moment to brush some snow off the branches that had dragged along the ground and left it outside. With cheeks pinched by the cold, I stepped in and pulled off my boots. The thick wool socks slipped off too, as socks do. I pulled them on again and grabbed a pair of slippers. Just like at Alma's house, my slippers were waiting for me at the door.

How I longed to see her again. Yearning took hold of my heart. Mom had called and said that they'd landed after some delay due to the fog at Heathrow and that they would get in around ten o'clock. Alma and her family would arrive tomorrow. Just the thought of Alma warmed my soul. A follow-up so soon after our last time together was nothing but luxury. It was nice to have a prompt continuation instead of waiting another year for the next chapter. I loved it.

Blasts from the past flashed by. I could clearly see it all, as if it were happening right now in front of me: Alma and me speeding down a hill on the old sled that had belonged to her grandmother. Ice skating on the lake. Getting lost in the woods. Grandma bringing a basket of afternoon snacks to us, deep in a snow cave that we had decorated with sprigs of fir trees and sheepskin. Freshly baked *kanelbullar*, hot chocolate, and Alma in a show hut. Maybe life would never get better than that.

* * *

Amid my Christmas decorating, with *lussebullar* baking, fatigue hit me like a knockout punch. There was no use fighting — I had already lost the match. Looking through a copy of the Christmas magazine *Julstämning* from 1983, my eyelids became as heavy as bowling balls.

I awoke to an uncomfortable sensation in my chest. A second later, I jumped up from the sofa as a screeching ringtone filled the whole room. My heart pounded with such intensity, I had to press my palm against my chest to try and calm myself. The phone continued to ring, cruelly in the silence. I was soaking wet with sweat. I took a few clumsy steps towards the hallway.

My foot had fallen asleep and couldn't fully carry my half-awake body. I stumbled and knocked over a stack of boxes filled with Christmas tree ornaments and tinsel. The scolding ring from the phone pushed in between my ribs and out through the house's coarse wooden siding. I couldn't find the phone in the dark, so it kept ringing and ringing.

Then it went dead silent. The darkness scared me. The quiet — mushrooming inside me — scared me. The woods outside scared me. My own heartbeat scared me. The fear scared me. I was shaking. The surging panic completely swept over me. Fear took hold. Lost and alone in the dark, I wanted to pull the emergency brake. I regained my calm for a few seconds, and I found the light switch. It took a few deep breaths until my eyes adjusted to the light.

I slid down on the floor, completely drained. Something was not right. Something… Then the ringing started again.

My body shook as I put the phone to my ear. I heard my voice as if it were someone else's. It didn't sound like Felicia Fanny Äng. I didn't sound like me at all.

Näsby Castle, Sweden

Around the same time

Ulrike, Alma's mother, was home alone and standing in the kitchen. The twins, Hugo and Eulalia, were at their grandparents' in Vallentuna, a twenty-minute drive away. They were five years old and had the Christmas jitters, as only children that age could. They were watching SVT's *Christmas Calendar* as it counted down with daily episodes until December 24th.

Ulrike stopped and realized Bruno wasn't home yet. She double-checked the calendar by the fridge. The bridge club from the Falken co-op association had their regular meetup at the café yesterday, so there wouldn't be much dirty dishes to deal with tonight, especially so close to Christmas. Bruno very rarely missed the evening news at six.

Where was the familiar sound on the front steps as he kicked off the fresh snow?

An antique Mora clock pierced the quiet with its ticking. When the clock on the stove said 06:06 PM in red, she didn't hesitate and rushed in a pair of *träskor* clogs to find him, storming into the café — ready for the worst.

Bruno was motionless on the sofa, staring into empty space with his boots and jacket on. He jolted as soon as he saw her, was almost like she had pulled him from a nightmare.

"Ulrike!" he called out in relief, as they joined in an embrace. "My heart really hurt. I had to sit down for a moment."

"Do you need help? Does it still hurt?" she asked as calmly as she could.

"No, it doesn't hurt. The pain went away. Sit with me for a bit. I'm so sorry if I scared you."

The Christmas lights strung on the bare cherry tree outside shone in the dense dark. The children's presents were already purchased. The bags were packed for their trip. It was Christmas after all, the stuff of fairytales. As soon as Alma came home, they would all go to grandma and grandpa in Vallentuna and pick up the twins. If Alma had caught the 06:10 PM train, she would be home any minute now.

Holding hands in silence, Bruno and Ulrike sat together on the sofa until Ulrike suddenly remembered the buns in the oven and ran back into the house. It had that scent of Christmas. Bruno was wrapping presents to the sound of Christmas carols when someone rang the doorbell. Two uniformed police officers were standing at the front door. A mother's scream pierced the cold winter night.

* * *

Bruno made a phone call that he wished would go unanswered. He let it ring and took a deep and grateful breath when no one picked up. The second time he got through, and I was the one who answered.

Mom and Dad followed my footsteps in the snow and found me just in my socks, next to the swing in the pine, oblivious of the cold.

* * *

The crosswalk signal had switched to green. Alma had stepped out into the street on her way to catch the 06:10 PM train from Östra Station when a driver ran the red light on Valhallavägen street. An ambulance had arrived within minutes.

It had been eighteen years since Ulrike rode in a wheelchair at Danderyds Hospital. Eighteen years since she cradled newborn Alma, as she was wheeled from the delivery room to a recovery room. Eighteen years since the bundle of life she'd held in her arms was no more than an hour old.

Eighteen years since the beginning of a life that was now over.

Her life had not been saved.

Alma was dead.

Hälsingland province, Sweden

The days that followed

Reality spares no one. But as long as I didn't write about it in the diary, it hadn't happened.

It didn't happen.

This isn't happening.

Nothing happened.

But it had happened. I just couldn't get the words on paper. The pen didn't have the vocabulary for it. The blue ink refused to write the black words.

It was dark and icy outside. The wind was blowing hard, spiky snowflake missiles. It was not a good night to be on the road. We decided to try to get some sleep — or at least rest — and drive to Näsby Allé the following morning, the day before Christmas Eve. But what did it matter? Christmas had been wiped away. It had lost everything it had ever meant. It would no longer be Christmas, just a regular shitty Tuesday that was anything but ordinary.

The old-fashioned wood-burning stove crackled. I found peace for a fragmented minute and dreamed of fireside reading — but then Bruno's nightmare phone call came back to me. I didn't want to sleep because I was afraid to wake up in my new reality. I felt so alone in the world. Slowly, my world faded into a dozy existence. Reality spares no one. Before I even opened my eyes, it was there and welcomed me into hell. And it haunted my nightmares. I couldn't tell if I'd gotten an ounce of sleep or if I just laid there and cried, blew my nose, and cried even more.

A tote bag from the Stadsmissionen charity store hung from a hook on the wall. The gift from Bruno was in it. His words still hung in the air. *It's a series of photographs named Belle Amie, from the ship docked in Stocksund where Alma goes to school... You are beautiful friends for life... You are each other's port, always will be.*

I wasn't sure what to do. Would it be stupid to open it? Perhaps it was wiser to wait to help get me through my sorrow later?

I peeled open the gift's elegant wrapping. Within another layer of tissue paper were three framed black-and-white photographs. Bruno had developed them in his darkroom. The first photo teleported me back to the day I met Alma. We were sitting at the water's edge with a box of strawberries between us. I was wearing shorts and a T-shirt and had just lost a tooth that I had put in a tiny wooden box with *My Baby Teeth* on the lid. The merry gap in my grin shone with the tooth's absence. The next photo, dated 1988 on the back, had caught yet another historic day in our friendship: We were standing with our summer dresses and sandals at Jontas Burgers! Alma held a package — no, not a package, I realized it was the binder, Amelia! She held it like a high school student on her way to math class in an American movie.

Although a little out of focus in the third photograph — I could see the binder sitting on the table behind us as Alma and I skipped out of Jontas burger joint, holding hands, swinging our arms in lyrical harmony.

If I could only defrost memories frozen in time. I was overcome with an urge to go to Alma's apartment. I wanted to be in her living room, where we had started to plan our journey — still small, like a newborn fire with smoke we were just beginning to sense. But the flames had been extinguished with the macabre power of an executioner. I doubted that even the toughest match could ever reignite it.

At half-past three, in the pitch dark night, I wanted to speak to Ulrike. I wanted to help mend a broken mother's heart. When I dialed her number in the morning, neither of us could comprehend how we had survived our first night without Alma. The world was in its sixteenth hour without her. We mostly cried. I told her we would leave after breakfast. Ulrike, with her heart open, said they would see us when we got to Näsby Allé. And then she thanked me for everything.

There was a knock at the door as soon as I hung up the phone.

"Good morning," Dad said and sat down next to me.

"No, Dad. It's not a good morning. Those no longer exist. They're gone forever."

There were no words that could comfort me, so we sat quietly. Our breathing became in sync.

"This is for you," Dad said. "I was going to wait and give it to you as a graduation gift. But I think you should have it now."

For a few silent seconds, I wondered if Dad was worried that he would lose me too. Was that why he was giving his gift now?

"Thanks, Dad."

I immediately recognized the fountain pen he placed in my hand. My Grandmother had given it to him after he had graduated high school. She was very ill at the time but had been given special permission from her doctor to attend the ceremony. Among everything he owned, the pen was the most precious. He never went anywhere without it.

"You have to write," Dad whispered. "You have to write."

"Are you sure? I know how much this pen means to you."

"Here's the ink," he said. "After a while, 'the helpers' will come to you. They're tiny, invisible creatures that'll help you find the words you need to understand life."

* * *

Dad always diligently took notes in the margins of whatever he was reading. He'd also cut pages out of magazines. When my parents lived in Casablanca, before I was born, his good friend had offered him a whole stack of blank diaries, which he gratefully accepted. Just before our trip to Hälsingland, Dad pulled out yet another diary, which became number thirty-two in the series. Every trip, a new diary: a unique story, a colorful cavalcade of dashes and dots on maps he pasted in with his notes, along with coffee-stained receipts, train tickets, and Polaroid shots.

Dad always said that like life itself, traveling was about replenishing your mind, soul, and body. Like the waves on a beach that didn't reach your toes, some moments on the road barely registered as memories. But then there were tsunami force instances sweeping me away for days until I could regain my footing. If I wasn't careful, I'd end up lost on the open sea, where not even the calming harbor of Alma could help.

Like that one night in Egypt when I was about thirteen. We had visited Alexandria on the Mediterranean up north, sleeping in timeless style at the Windsor Palace Hotel along the Corniche waterfront promenade. From there, we had flown to see the landmark Karnak temple in Luxor. I had felt so small amongst the grandest buildings of Ancient Egypt. We rode a *felucca* on the Nile. We jumped on a train to Aswan, known for its dam, and then took a bus at dawn for Abu Simbel to watch the sunrise over the massive rock temples carved out of the mountain.

We were finishing up our ten-day trip with a couple of nights in Giza, close to the great pyramids. I was alone in the apartment where we were staying. It belonged to a family friend, and Mom was out shopping for tomorrow's breakfast. The darkness had settled, and I was enjoying a moment of reflection on the roof terrace with a full view of the great pyramids, sipping *karkade*, tea made from hibiscus flower petals.

My pencil danced across the diary pages, leaving words in its trace. Dad joined me when he got back from his solo visit to the Egyptian Museum in Cairo. He turned the page of his travel journal to a drawing of the golden mask of Pharaoh Tutankhamun. Discovered by British archaeologist Howard Carter in the Valley of the Kings in 1925, the mask was a three-thousand-year-old work of art.

"The Egyptians fill the graves with artifacts for the afterlife," Dad said. "Tools, amulets — things to prepare for what happens later, so to say."

I was still blissfully unaware of where this conversation would take me emotionally. He continued:

"Felicia, you know the camping stool that's always strapped to my backpack?"

"Yeah, Dad. The one you use when you draw?"

"Yes, that one. I'd like to bring it with me when it's time to go."

I didn't fully understand. So, he put his hand on mine, and the truth knocked me over.

"When I die, then I'd like to take it to heaven."

* * *

I dug into oblivion in search of memories. Spotted countless scenes in my mind, everything Alma and I experienced together. I remembered so many strange moments. Memories bombarded me, like meteorites from all directions. Settling in the past numbed my heart from the despair that had me in an iron grip. It helped me collect more sunrises.

I was struck by the most mundane things that had changed. I would never write her address on an envelope again, receive one of her letters, or eat hummus with her. When a human died, an entire library disappeared. Alma's life had lasted 6,408 days. If I had known our breakfast in Näsby Allé would be our last together, would I have grabbed one more coffee? Said something I had never told her? Maybe I would have held onto the hug for a few more seconds and turned around before the train closed its doors, screaming how much I loved her?

I took a quick peek into my room just before we left the lake house. I left the bedroom door wide open behind me. I was the last one out of the house. I locked the front door behind me one final time. *Goodbye lake house*, I whispered, *I don't think I can ever come back again*. It was a parallel sadness I had to put aside for now. I had no room for more grief.

Unlike all other times we'd left, I didn't look back when we crested up over the hill. It would have hurt too much. I sat in the back seat behind my mom with the travel journal I had bought the day Amelia returned to us. I held my dad's pen — my pen now. As we came out on the main road, courage finally took hold, and the tip touched the paper. One by one, the words came. A little teasing at first, shy, but then they flowed on. They were like tears in sadness, waves of laughter during joy, or the kisses and caresses when you're in love. Dad had been right. "The helpers" had stood by my side and would never leave me.

Like a long line of dancers, the words linked arms to one another and moved across the pages in new formations that had never been seen before. When the music ended, and the last dance was done, my palm was sweaty and damp from holding the pen for so long. I had let my thoughts rejoice as if no one could see their shy dance in the dark. And in that dark — for the first time since Bruno's phone call — I saw the sun breaking in the winter landscape. A tiny little ray was warming up the frozen ground, and it was now slowly thawing. A small bud burst out of the ground and said hello.

Sweden swept past the car window, like a Svealand documentary on fast forward. The stunning winter landscape with all the dreams behind the lace curtains in the living rooms. All the existence we passed in our rental car, all the feelings, all the desire. All the life, and all the death, along the way. People who wanted to renovate their deck, raise children, repaint the fence, call a good friend, book trips to Mallorca, go to the library, move abroad, pick the kids up from the swimming pool, go to the post office, write a book... All the little big things that made life so wonderful, unique, beautiful. And so painful.

* * *

We slowed to the thirty kilometers per hour speed limit as we turned right onto the lane that led to Näsby Castle. I counted the trees that lined the road like I always did. There were more than a hundred. I wished the road would never end; that we would never arrive at the inevitable reality awaiting at the destination. We were thankfully held up a few more minutes when the barriers at the railroad crossing dropped. There was the familiar howl of the train. Dad parked just outside the castle gates.

I opened the car door, but it was so overwhelming I couldn't go on. I was choking and had to get fresh air in my system. Lots of it. I ran out onto a barren football field, through thickets and bushes that were hard and nasty from the winter and snow. They scratched my face. I screamed to the hollow sky. Through the leafless trees down at the water, I caught the icy sea and wanted nothing but to disappear into it forever. I collapsed, flat on the ground like a wingless snow angel. Shivering and screaming. I didn't know what to do. When would I ever recognize myself? I vomited from the crushing uncertainty.

Mom and Dad helped me to my feet. Ulrike approached us with a blanket that she put over my shoulders. Together we formed a circle in the middle of the field. I lifted my eyes to the cold sky.

Was she up there? I wanted to scream the question as loud as possible: Are you up there? If not, where can I find you? An ice cream truck played its happy jingle, but nothing was like it used to.

* * *

I crossed Djursholmsvägen road with Alma's apartment key in my hand. When Alma's kitchen window came into my view, I grabbed hold of a nearby fence to support myself. There was light from a lamp somewhere inside. I entered the door code — 1819 — it felt as if the universe was making a cruel joke to remind me Alma would never be nineteen.

I took in the staircase with its light gray color with confetti flakes in blue and yellow cascades. The garbage chute. *Tie your trash bags closed.* The carpet in front of her door that said, *Stay away if you're not nice.* The door that Alma would never open again. I fumbled with the key. Trembling, I dropped it on the floor. As I picked it up, I hoped it wouldn't fit. Here and now, I wanted to wake up from the nightmare that had darkened everything with its black curtain. And yet the reality was worse than any bad dream. Maybe there would be a new tenant, I thought. They would have already carried their moving boxes up the stairs, and their kids would be running on the parquet floor. Happy baby steps. The key slipped into the lock and turned. No locksmith had changed it. Everything was like it was before and yet, not. The door opened.

There was ringing as my coat brushed the bells hanging by the coat rack. The apartment still smelled of Alma but wouldn't for much longer. I took off my shoes and put on the slippers that were still there. My slippers. In the hall sat the round carpet that Alma's grandmother Anna-Karin had woven. The simple red vase now had a twig of ivy in it.

Light shone from the electric Advent candles in the kitchen. The ivy on the windowsill was a little dry and the leaves had begun to wilt. I watered it. Alma's dining table and chairs, the hyacinth, and Christmas decorations she had been in the middle of making. In her bedroom — where no one would make love anymore — the bed cover had been light-heartedly thrown over the bed. The glass for the toothbrushes was upside down. Alma's toiletries were packed for Christmas in Hälsingland. Inside the living room, the wide silk fabrics still hung from the ceiling, but the warmth of their colors had become cold.

I shivered. I had never felt this far from home before. Without Alma, this was all just a shell. Walls, floors, and ceilings. Without Alma, it was nothing. I thought I would suffocate. What was left of the hot dog that I had managed to eat on the drive here came back up. I cried like a child who had fallen hard on asphalt, the first tumble of spring. The sun was making an exit, and heavy darkness started slipping over everything in the apartment.

Alma was just out to the grocery store and would soon be back with a carton of milk and *Kexchoklad* chocolate bars. Or she was taking out the trash or renting a movie. At the library maybe? She was late, met a friend and got carried away. Maybe an unscheduled session with her therapist. It just couldn't be this way; she would be back soon. This is not how it should be.

Tears made everything look like a blurry film, but the emotions were in clear black-and-white. I wanted to run from here. Alma's scent had become a stench that stung my nose and cut into my heart each time the fumes greeted my conscience. I sat down on the floor and cried uncontrollably. A cry no one could comfort. Because there was no consolation, there were no solutions. The realization that everything had forever and irrevocably changed was absolutely devastating. My sight went dark. Maybe my eyes had finally given up.

That's when the mail slot in the door opened and slammed shut. I jumped up. Had I been asleep? Had I been dreaming? Why was the post being delivered so late in the afternoon?

I crawled over on all fours. On the doormat lay a Christmas postcard with a hot pink Post-it note plastered over Santa Claus. I leaned against the front door in shock.

Hi Alma!

The postman mistakenly delivered your postcard to me. Here it is, better late than never.

Merry Christmas!

- Sigrid, one floor down.

I held in my hand our promise. The one we had pinky sworn to do on December 18th, just a few days earlier.

...it's always fun to get a letter, even when you expect it!...

* * *

This was Alma's doing. Even from the dead, she reminded me what I had come here for. I ran to the living room. The binder was inside the cabinet by the window, and I brought it to the kitchen.

I slid the tip of a wooden letter opener under the tab that Alma had licked shut eight years earlier and tore it open. It was a postcard-sized envelope with a bulge in the middle. Whatever had been in there for so many years gave a rattling noise.

Hi Felicia,

You're my very best friend.

I'm sitting in my secret hiding place as I write this letter to you. I hope you will read this when you are a very old lady! You'll be in a rocking chair with funny glasses and a checkered blanket across your knees, like my great aunt.

I was only eighteen and at least seventy years from being *very old*. I would never become an old lady, that was something others thought you were! The words fused on the paper as my tears dripped onto the *vaxduk* tablecloth. I turned around for some paper towels to blow my nose.

I sometimes think it's so sad that best friends can't go to each other's funerals. So, if I die before you, then I'm lucky because then you can come to my funeral when you are a very old lady.

I want you to do something for me at my funeral, so it won't be so terribly sad. Because I know how people just cry and wear black clothes.

I took a deep breath, glanced over the Advent candles and out the window, and then went back to reading.

* * *

I clinked my fork against my glass and waited as coffee cups were carefully placed on the sterile white linen cloths with vague floral patterns. My legs shook with all the eyes in the parish house dining room directed at me. Would I keep my voice from breaking?

"I want to say a few words, at Alma's request," I said. "Alma wrote this when she was nine years old. She put it in an envelope, which we put in a binder that traveled the world and returned to us just a few days before Alma died. It's a long and amazing story, but one for another time."

I smiled. My voice hadn't cracked. Like a presenter at a Hollywood awards show, I took Alma's letter out of the envelope. I felt all of the looks on me and the heat on my cheeks blushing. She had been gone just over three weeks. 1996 had shaken hands with 1997 at midnight eight days earlier. I thought about the solemn funeral ceremony. Everything in white. The flowers, the coffin, the flickering candles.

"So these are Alma's words that I am about to read."

Hi, everyone, please don't cry.

You are the best friends and family in the whole wide world. By now, we will have known each other for a really long time. Maybe we share a thousand million memories?

I looked over at Bruno, who was holding Ulrike's hand in his. I continued reading:

I like my mom and dad so much. But they probably died a long time ago because mothers and fathers die before their children. Sometimes I read in the newspaper or see on TV that a girl has died in a car accident, and then I get really sad and wonder why and how her mother is feeling.

If you are already dead, I can tell you when we meet in heaven, and if you are still alive, thank you, Mom and Dad, for being so kind. Thanks for all the strawberries in the summers, our road trips, and all the Friday dinners of yummy spaghetti and meat sauce. I don't think fish sticks are very tasty, but lemonade and cinnamon buns are delicious.

Ulrike squeezed Bruno's hand, hard. He looked up at the ceiling, out the window, and then down at the table and wiped his eyes. I wondered if Bruno's weak heart could cope with today? Someone blew their nose, another sneezed.

I cleared my throat and felt my confidence grow within me. No one had been prepared for Alma's death. We were experiencing something in that moment, together, that we could not have imagined ever happening before then. This moment was unique to all of us. It had never happened and would never happen again. In that knowledge, I found a humbling clarity that I was doing us all a favor and giving us weapons in the war against grief.

My funeral!

I can't believe I'm dead! Can you? How did it happen?

Felicia is there. I'm sure because otherwise, you wouldn't hear what I wrote in this letter! If she can read, of course, she is surely very old and has glasses and a big funnel in her ear and may not be able to walk and see very well. Does she have a cane? Please make sure she doesn't forget and leave it afterwards! Thanks. Otherwise, she might be going home without it. She might be a hundred years old. How old did I get?

I am nine years old today as I write this, so I imagine it has been maybe eighty years. Is it about 2067? What does the world look like now? Some of you may not even remember me, because I know that old people often forget many things. So, I'll tell you.

My name is Alma, and I want to be an adventurer. When I grow up, I'll buy a hot air balloon and go wherever I want, just like Amelia Earhart. I will go to every country on the planet — from Afghanistan to Zimbabwe.

Here I had to take a break. A sip of water. A deep breath.

I hope my best friend Felicia can come with me, at least to some places in the alphabet, let's say A, C, J, and S. America, Cuba, Japan, Sweden + Spain! She is my best friend, and when you hear this we will have traveled the world together.

I paused.

A minute of silence? I wondered.

There was a lump of sadness in my throat, like a bump in the road. Must slow down. One deep breath later, I managed to change gears and hit the gas.

If you look up into the sky, you will see my hot air balloon. It is red and green and blue and yellow.

Wave to me!

All the funeral guests turned to the window, where the sunbeams were streaming in as if on command. It was like Alma had moved some clouds around to shine some light on the January darkness. A collective sense of wonder swept through the room.

Wave, I said!

And then everyone waved.

Now I will close shut the envelope. Think of me when the sun shines because that's what we do up here to dry tears.

See you!

"Hugo. Eulalia," I said. The twins were sitting next to each other and playing with the dessert spoons. They weren't surprised like everyone else when I said their names. We had gone over the plan together days before.

PS:

Each of you will now receive something, so you never forget me.

With love always,

Alma Lindgren

In a blazer and khaki-colored chinos, Hugo picked a basket up from under the table and walked up to Bruno.

Eulalia, with her dark red dress and also carrying a basket, directed her steps towards Ulrike.

"Here you go, Dad," said Hugo. "This is from Alma!"

"Mom, this is for you. I love you," said Eulalia.

They walked in opposite directions along the long table and around the room, handing out packets of seeds, the same kind that Alma had included in her letter. The twins met at the end of the room and returned, hand-in-hand to their seats. The room swirled with murmuring as I reached my grand finale.

"Sow these forget-me-not seeds in Alma's memory. May they bloom each spring. Thank you," and I raised my glass. "To absent friends!"

Sunlight streaming in through the windows reflected off the clinking glasses like it was dancing the jitterbug on the walls. Ulrike thanked everyone for coming, and guests started to form a long line to bid Alma's family farewell. When everyone had left, Bruno lowered himself into the family car's front passenger seat. Alma's godmother Hedvig Eleonora was driving them all back home to Näsby Allé. Every seat in the Lindgren car was filled as usual. Today, there could be no echoing black hole between the twins in the back.

I looked off into a nearby field, snowy and edged with trees. A pair of deer ran across the white planes in joyful jolts, and, for a brief moment, the spell of my aching loneliness was broken.

London, England

Beginning of 1997

A week after Alma's funeral, a seatbelt was strapped across my waist, and I was on my way back to London. One last spring term awaited me. The final stretch before I graduated. Within a few weeks, letters and emails from top-ranked schools with renowned political science departments in the United States would start to arrive and announce if they wanted me. But I had completely different plans.

The tears became uncontrollable as Sweden dwindled under the wings and then disappeared below the clouds. A trip that had started with helium balloons and tulips at Arlanda airport had ended with shopping at Åhléns department store for black clothes to wear to a funeral.

For the umpteenth time, I looked through the travel journal I had bought a few days before Christmas when life was colorful. The first line read *OUR JOURNEY*. I had written it while waiting for Alma to come back home that day, but now I was unsure of what to do with the word *OUR*. I left it, even though I was solo now.

Underneath it, I had noted the following:

New York: Marathon in November, same month as Mrs. Hewson's birthday. What if I go then? New York, New York!

Sweden: Selma Björling and her big family at Hämma Manor. Beautiful in summer. Would love to visit the legendary province of Dalarna — it literally means 'the valleys.' Sounds like the stuff of fairy tales.

Japan: Yuzuki Sato, either in Spring or Autumn. I've heard so much about sakura! I would love to see Japan.

Cuba: Clara Santos, the seamstress in Santiago de Cuba.

Barcelona: Rosana Mundi has an apartment with a spare room I can use for as long as I want to stay.

On the next page, I had started to organize the locations. As I looked over it again, it struck me that they all fit into a single handy route. If I started with Selma Björling in Sweden in July-August, traveled south to Spain, then across the Atlantic to America, made a quick side trip to Cuba, then went to Japan, my and Alma's dream would be real: a trip around the world. Just that it was solo, Amelia Earhart style.

I had about six months to plan the whole adventure, and I had already completed the scariest part: telling Mom and Dad. I quietly reveled in my victory. I had released the truth inside me, Felicia Fanny Äng. My dreams were mine and only mine. They didn't go hand-in-hand with my family's chosen routes of academia and prestigious job titles. I had decided to go my own way. I would travel my own journey.

Maybe they thought my path was a detour, a typo, or something that could be course-corrected with repeated arguments about the importance of a college degree. In their minds, a good school opened doors, but I saw brighter possibilities lining up along a path I was yet to walk. My life journey, the journey of my life.

For the first time since Alma died, the future had something good about it. And I had goosebumps.

New York City Marathon, 1997

I can do this.

The start.

The first step — always the hardest.

Staten Island.

The speakers blare out Frank Sinatra's ode to New York City. Papa-daba-daaaa papa-da-ba-daaaaaaa papa-dabada duuuuuuu…

I can do this.

It's like a concert when they just open the gates to let everyone in. The sound of the crowd rises from the field ahead. It's crowded. Energy bounces around inside of me. I jump up and down, see the bobbing heads far ahead of me. As the masses move forward, I can slowly start to take a few steps onto the abutment for Verrazano-Narrows Bridge. A little at a time, the field opens up enough to run at a comfortable pace. I can keep it like this for four hours, without giving up.

I can do this.

The skyscrapers cut into the clear blue sky like razor blades. In the distance, I can see the Statue of Liberty. She's quite small in her large glory, where she stands facing Manhattan.

And I am going to make it here today. It's up to me, New Me New Me.

Jackets, gloves, and hats are scattered all over the road. I lose myself in the ocean of people. I'm part of the larger mass with the same goal.

Runners stop and take photos. Some guys piss through the bridge rail.

My legs trot on. I am a mare with the energy of a stallion. Heel strike, midfoot, toe off, heel strike, midfoot, toe off. Over and over and over again. Heel strike, midfoot, toe off, heel strike, midfoot, toe off. Over and over and over again. Again, and again.

The sun is shining and there's no breeze. Brooklynites proudly welcome us as we come across the bridge like it's the Rio Carnival. I'm swept into a simmering atmosphere of intensity. There's a little girl offering orange slices. I take one and feel its juicy nourishment.

Right foot, left foot; right, left. I wonder how many steps I'll run. Right foot, left foot; right, left.

One hundred thousand, maybe?

Climbing up the steep inclines of the bridges, my steps increase and become shorter, heavier, and heavier, and... heavier.

A girl stretches her calf against a stop sign. *WALK* flashes on the traffic light next to her. A man rubs Vaseline on his thighs. Another runner, older, falls flat on his face, but it only leaves him with scrapes on his knees and holes in his gloves. Someone from the crowd hands him band-aids.

It feels like an improvised story with everyone playing their own leads and background characters at the same time. A drama. A thriller. A nailbiter. A comedy. Reality TV in reality.

New York, New York.

New Felicia, New Me.

I cool off by running in the shade of some buildings and hit high-fives from the crowd like dominoes. The emotions of everything overwhelm me. Someone passes me a paper towel, which comes in handy when the tears and snot start to flow.

At the water and aid station, I slow down to walk and drink. Pour out what's left. Throw out the empty paper cup. Run on. The more I slow down, the harder it is to get started again. It's easier to run than walk, easier than stopping.

Is that how outrunning grief works too?

Pushing forward instead of lying down, slowing down?

Is it best to decide on how far to go before you can rest?

I read *"I am Sam"* on the back of a T-shirt on a man walking in a way that's more like limping, with one helper on each side. A third person is right behind them, pushing his empty wheelchair. "Go Sam!" I yell out.

How many hours will it take him to get to Central Park?

A tough uphill in Brooklyn takes all the energy out of me. It's my first real moment of weakness. Frustration and fatigue come over me. One foot at a time. The only way forward is through it. A fact so overwhelmingly annoying. A piece of chocolate from an older lady with lovely curves helps me through that crisis. I turn into a missile.

There's a soundtrack.

It has such a rhythm.

It has such speed.

Such tempo.

I hopscotch between cultures, languages, and atmospheres. I'm running through the best of Cuban, rock, gospel, salsa, soul, hip-hop. I hear cowbells, drums, and hoorays in all the world's languages.

"Come on!"

"Looking good!"

"Come on now!"

"¡*Vamos España!*"

"*Heja Sverige!*" from a few fellow countrymen waving blue and yellow flags.

I'm surprised at the good pace I'm keeping. I'm running at about six minutes per kilometer, and it's a piece of cake. Simple to calculate from there. Ten kilometers per hour. The whole marathon is just four cakes and an extra small pastry. A Swedish pastry? A little *semla*. I get the marzipan munches! A *mazarin*! That would be absolutely divine at a time like this. I remember my first *mazarin* ever with Bruno and Alma at the Östermalmshallen food market on an excursion to Stockholm. The almond paste, coated in sugar.

The sense of loss overwhelms me. I want to run away from it. So, I move on. With Alma light like an angel on my shoulder.

Dalarna province, Sweden

Summer of 1997

The journey had begun, and I was consumed by the serene beauty. The province was a peaceful green with the traditional *falu* red of Swedish family cabins spread through it like confetti. The mountains, with rooftops sprinkled all the way up, crested into a pine forest at the top. Sleepy meadows rolled down towards the river.

Will you grow here, sheltered from the wind? I asked Alma's forget-me-not seeds as I put them in the lush soil. I tried to imagine the petals of blue Post-its that would caress our hearts in the summertime, to make the living easier. Almost eight months had passed since Alma died.

My even-footed landing from the train onto the platform was the first time I ever set foot in Dalarna. Selma Björling came and picked me up at the Leksand train station. We headed south in her blue Volvo station wagon and passed signs warning of *Children at Play* on either side of the curvy road, like they were gates in a slalom competition. Surely no children would die in a place as idyllic as this, where branches of apple trees hung temptingly over fences. We crossed a bridge, turned onto a smaller road, and honked a greeting to a neighbor. I stretched my neck to see past the hood as we drove up and over a shy hill. The road flattened out into a lane lined with stately birches that gave shade over the earth, dry and hot from summer.

"Welcome to Hämma Manor," said Selma as she parked the car next to an old, log cabin-like building. It was a *bagarstuga* — once used for baking bread and now an architectural artifact. A little girl with braids ran towards me at top speed and gave me a bear hug.

"Hej Felicia, I am Tilda!" she said and pulled me to a playhouse under a rowan tree.

Tilda served me imaginary coffee in a miniature tea set. When I was full and content, I walked to the main house and up a big staircase. The door to Tilda's room, where I would stay, was open. A Swedish flag swayed against the calm summer sky. They had hoisted it for me. My arrival was a celebration, and I had made a new best friend already. Tilda was the youngest at Hämma Manor but had been there longest.

* * *

My dad — when preparing for our Christmas holiday in Sweden — had taken the Tube to Charing Cross Road to spend a few hours in Foyles. He headed for the travel section and, without hesitation, pulled out a book called *On the Road: A Swedish Love Story.* Tucked in amongst a massive thirty miles of shelves — longer than a marathon, with a listing in Guinness World of Records — was a book whose fabric I would be woven into. It was about a British couple spending a few months traveling through Sweden. They met another couple, two married doctors, while hiking the Kungsleden trail near the border with Norway. The doctors were described as residents of Hämma Manor, originally from Umeå up north.

Hämma Manor had been added to my path thanks to the Amelia binder flying into Selma's warm embrace. But the story of the house where I would sleep that night had made its way to me before we had even met. Maybe it was just the simple magic of stories. I immediately knew the perfect gift to bring for Selma and Anton. I only had to wrap *On the Road: A Swedish Love Story* in a piece of textile from Morocco.

* * *

Good-hearted ghosts allegedly inhabited the attic at Hämma Manor. They came down the stairs and pulled on aprons every so often, especially around Saint Lucia day in December. Sometimes the porcelain figurines on display in the cabinets changed direction. I noticed them looking at me. A deer, a rabbit, and a horse. Did they move as I walked around the room? Everything that could ever be preserved at the manor was left as it was. There was such a sense of the past. Who had chosen all the paintings, carpets, and clocks that represented another time? What histories did they tell of the friendly ghosts?

On the grand tour of the manor, Selma showed me around to the dining room and the parlor on the ground floor. The plush couch in the salon was purple and rubbed rough against my bare legs when they moved against its grain. Selma's favorite space was the eastward-facing morning room where she planned her day — meetings, purchases — after the sun rose on Hämma Manor. All the phone calls with social workers and people from child services were made there as well.

Sheepskin vests and long coats on wormwood hangers hung out in the cloakroom. The dress shoes and Charleston outfits from the roaring twenties were *to die for* — which is what I cried out in awe — even though I had made a conscientious effort not to use that phrase since Alma left us.

"All these dresses were brought back from America, and there are a ton more up in the attic! Some pretty progressive owners have lived here if I may say," Selma laughed.

The 1920s — the Jazz Age — was a joyful era when many women found their footing. (I had written all about it in a paper and included some parts in my high school graduation speech.) Amelia Earhart found more than her footing. She found the skies — showing the way that I would eventually walk, run, and fly myself.

"Before I leave Hämma Manor, I'd love to try them on. I want to see how it feels to wear all these dresses."

And just like that, I planned my first activity, exactly in line with the advice from my therapist to *try to stay active without overdoing it*. In the dresses, shoes, and jewelry brought back from Charleston to Sweden seventy years earlier, I could impersonate iconic women before me, who were fortunate to prosper in an era sandwiched between World War I and the Great Depression.

* * *

Selma took me around to the courier room where the post, groceries, and fresh produce from local farms were delivered once upon a time. Here, they lived as in the past. It was like I had been dropped into a bygone era that was still more alive than ever. What if... I had been born a hundred years before?

Selma and Anton had kept the wood stove in the kitchen, along with copper pots and ladles, jammed together and packed in a large clay pot, eager to whip up some soup. The beds were so high they gave panoramic views through the windows of Lake Siljan without having to lift one's head from the floral pillows embroidered with some unknown relative's initials. A linen room on the second floor was filled with tablecloths, pillowcases, and bed sheets that smelled of lavender, roses, and grandmothers. Back when the house had been built in the early 1900s, the huge bathtub had to be filled by servants hauling buckets of hot water from the kitchen. The grand tour completed, we sat down in the parlor with a cup of coffee and cookies that the kids had baked.

"I'm so sorry for your loss," Anton said. "We understand how much Alma meant to you." Then, after a moment, he added: "I lost my little brother, Milo. We spent the winter break in Sälen up north, and a week later, the doctors found a brain tumor."

Anton got up and handed me a framed photograph from a side table that I had noticed when Selma was showing me around. It had an aura of grief and had been kept next to a lit candle. Anton and Milo were laughing on either side of a snowman. They were dressed to go skiing, probably no more than nine or ten years old.

"We had the time of our lives," Anton said. "Our first-time skiing — nobody could stop us!"

* * *

I thanked Selma and Anton for *fika*, the Swedish equivalent of afternoon tea in London but with coffee, and went up to the room where I was staying. My backpack was on the floor, and I began to unpack it. I hung my clothes on pale pink padded hangers with little yellow bows that smelled of lavender. Tilda's clothes hung in the same wardrobe. It seemed like she didn't have many outfits. This was her last summer without a summer vacation. Selma would be taking her to her first day of school in August.

I pulled the curtain back and looked out onto the garden with its large rose bushes generously spreading pink in the surrounding green. There was a path down to the gate and the nearby river that could be seen between summer fresh birch leaves. It looked like diamonds had been sprinkled on the surface of the water. I closed the wardrobe door, left the room, and went out to explore what lay waiting for me down by the river's fighting current. Where the meadow met the edge of the beach, I planted Alma's seeds. Memories of her came back. I remembered song lyrics about the blue, blue sky and water, and flowers. It was a beautiful first day at Hämma Manor.

A cowbell rang, and I turned toward the main house. I took the path back through the gate, entering the yard and past the rose bushes. I followed a gravel walk that led towards the house beside a couple of small benches and imagined ladies sitting on them in pretty dresses with big collars, wasp waists, and stellar hats. Gesticulating over whisky sour, they would perfect their world takeover masterplan. One day, a woman would fly solo across the Atlantic. One day, the most powerful nation on the planet would have a woman President. One day... the future would have a place for me in it, and I navigated towards it.

Small fish swam among the water lilies in a large water fountain, inducing a sense of contemplation. Throwing a coin would never bring my Alma back, but I still tossed in fifty pence that had been in my jean pocket for a good while. It would be ages until I returned to London anyway. Had the priceless wishes sunk to oblivion or been fulfilled?

Selma waited on the veranda in front of a pair of wide-open large white-painted doors. The curtains swayed behind her. A homely smell of garlic tickled my hunger. The trip from Stockholm had taken just under four hours, including changing trains in Borlänge, and it had been a while since I had eaten anything substantial. A sandwich I'd bought just after we passed Uppsala had lasted through Heby, Sala, and Avesta Krylbo. Just before Hedemora, I walked through the train again to find the trolley selling snacks. I got a cup of tea, which I sipped while counting down the stations at Säter, Borlänge, Djurås, Gagnef, and Insjön.

"We're almost ready for dinner," Selma said. "You're gonna eat like a horse. You get like that here at Hämma Manor! Just wait to see how much the kids eat!"

Selma, so charming in the brightly colored pink-purple-blue-green Tricia Guild apron that my mother had bought for her in London. Her always inviting smile, her curly and bushy hair. Selma looked younger than her newly reached sixty years of age, which she told me had been marked with a fine celebration at Hämma Manor attended by almost a hundred guests, who'd come by train, car, and on foot.

Anton was in the kitchen, standing over the stove and stirring saucepans with enough spaghetti and meat sauce in them for the entire Leksand ice hockey team. Three coasters had been placed on the table, on which the dishes would constantly switch and trade places during dinner. Three carafes were lined up next to them — lemon and lime slices floating inside in calm symbiosis, like goldfish schooled in Zen.

The table was set for ten people, and one after another, kids and teenagers began to arrive. Harald, Julia, Robban, Fatima, Marko, Anastasia, and then my roommate Tilda with the braids. It was a lovely bunch. Beard stubble, vocal cords on the way into puberty voice changes, and just a bit too much eyeliner. And then little Tilda, so cute yet in contrast to the tough-looking guys and girls who were almost twice as old but equally kind.

Anton turned off the heat while still stirring the pasta, splashed it generously with olive oil and salt, poured it into three identical blue bowls, and then garnished it with a sprig of parsley Marko had brought in from the vegetable garden next to the playhouse.

Working in tandem, Selma and Anton oozed a love that was more palpable than the smell of garlic from the steaming meat sauce on the table in front of us. They had met at the Roskilde music festival, immediately became a couple, and married three months later. They were made for each other.

"Hey, everyone. Listen up for a second," Selma called out. "Before we start, let's say hi and welcome Felicia. She'll be here with us for a while."

"Hi Felicia!" everyone said in a disjointed cacophony.

"Are Selma and Anton your summer parents?" Tilda asked. She was sitting next to me with the floral paper napkin in her lap. I could tell from the state of her braids that she had been playing all day.

"No, not really. Selma is my friend. My parents live in London."

"Is London far away?"

"It is so far away that you have to drive in a car for a whole day, then ride on the boat for so long that you have to sleep on the boat, and go a little farther after you wake up."

"Oh, then you need a good car and a good boat too! My mom has no car."

"Or you can fly. Then it's faster, and you're there in a few hours."

Tilda's eyes lit up.

"I have never been on an airplane, but I think I will fly when I grow up. To the moon!"

Tilda, the solo pilot, was a real charmer. Another Amelia Earhart, maybe?

"Selma is not my mother, but she is *like* my mother. She is kind, and it's fun here. And when I start school, then Anton and Selma will help me with homework. And I can swim whenever I want and play with all the other kids."

"Then maybe we can play together later, after dinner? And read a fairy tale before we sleep."

"Yes, let's do that! I'll show you my favorite climbing tree. And where there are wild strawberries. And a bird's nest. And a nice stone that looks like a big beetle. And you and I can sleep in the same room, because there is a bunk bed, and there's no one sleeping on the top bunk right now, so I think you and I can be best friends."

Tilda was like Alma when we were kids, that summer day when she came with the strawberries. Her death still hit me relentlessly, even though its force had started to wane. With every breath, I inhaled grief, misery, and anger, but somehow, I still hadn't suffocated. I couldn't explain why living was even possible, given the civil war going on inside of me. Discouragement and despair had destroyed and colored everyday life with a hazy gray color scale. The palette had faded away. The pressure of misery pushing any good out of my head was deafening. It hurt the heart. But the days became weeks and months. Again, and again I had to ask: How. Was. It. Possible? Had someone pressed fast forward?

* * *

In London, after the funeral, I had spent all my time in the library, focused on my studies. I rewrote, corrected, and deleted entire papers, starting over from the beginning. Obsessed with keeping myself as busy as possible, I never left any glaring gaps in my calendar. When I wasn't plugging away at schoolwork, I ran. Several times a week. Sometimes even two or three times a day. That's how I managed it. That's how I survived the spring semester and graduated with forty-five credits, the highest total possible — which was almost unheard of — and with praise from all my teachers. For me, it was never about accomplishment. It was survival.

On paper, my spring term was a tremendous success. But, in fact, it was a disaster. So many emotions were compressed into my vacuum-packed self. I banned every outlet, banned empty minutes, forbade myself from feeling. I went to a psychologist but never did any of the exercises she recommended. My answers to her questions were pre-planned regurgitations of what she wanted to hear. It wasn't Felicia Fanny Äng who talked to her. It was someone else. I could try to flee from the memory of Alma and not think about her, but the hole drilled by her absence always left a space of nothing. I could never fill it, no matter what the material. And no matter how complex my escape route, it always led back to the same truth.

The weeks turned into months. Despite my grief blocking the buds from breaking, the unthinkable spring came. How did it dare welcome me into its new beginnings?

Mom, Dad, and I took the Eurostar train from Waterloo to Gare du Nord to spend the Easter holidays in Paris. I planted some seeds among the geraniums in the flower box that hung along our balcony at the Hôtel Baume near the Jardin du Luxembourg. Botanical patches of color that, after some time, would pop up and say, "Peek-a-boo!"

Paris in spring… Everyone seemed so happy and in love. I was neither. With the warm weather came a switch from shoes to sandals. My soul and soles were hurting. Even when the green grass tickled my toes as I walked home from school through the lush park halfway home, it didn't feel like it had before. When I lay in the sun with my books next to me — and with the splashing scent of grass playing in my nose — the sensations didn't reach where they used to in my brain. When I sat on a bench and saw people holding hands, I just felt nothing. Neither more, nor less. I wanted Alma back in my life so badly.

Was but a teaspoon of joy too much to ask for? I often thought to myself, always weighed down by sadness that I had to carry against my will forever.

* * *

In cities like Buenos Aires, Maputo, Stockholm, Beirut, Paris, and London, I had become an esteemed regular at bakeries, shops, and restaurants. Some owners had become friends for life — lifelines, at times offering help, like when I was locked out in Maputo, and the lady at the pharmacy served me snacks while she contacted the Swedish embassy and left a message for Mom. I knew that I had lived in places many would never visit even once in their lifetime. My everyday life was out of their reach.

"Pinch yourself," my dad would often say over a cup of chamomile tea. "Can you believe that we *live* here?" with an extra emphasis on *live*.

But none of that was of any help anymore. I lived, and I was alive, but so what? Eventually, a vague path forward started to form, leading me away from the epicenter of my existential crisis. It began with "Thanks. But no thanks" to the finest schools on the American east coast. I was going to travel, unknowing that my first destination would be at the hospitality of Selma, a caretaker of other people. A janitor, a guardian, a person of good. She gave life her all — repairing broken hearts and families — without expecting the slightest in return. Our paths had crossed so that my soul, broken into a thousand pieces, would be put back together. That, I figured, was why the Amelia binder had landed in her lap.

* * *

The book, *On the Road: A Swedish Love Story,* got us talking.

> *What had once been a Christmas gift for a young woman whose fiancé was an endless romantic had later become a summer retreat for a couple from Umeå, who were both doctors. They had no children. After their sudden deaths in a boating accident on a nearby lake sometime in the seventies, the manor had been left to*

decay. The window shutters were nailed shut and the front door locked for good.

"There is talk in the village that anyone who lives here will meet a tragic fate," Selma said, "and that there is a curse on Hämma Manor."

"The last member of the family that originally owned it and his wife remained childless and died when their hunting lodge burned to the ground," Anton added, "and the couple who moved in after them, the doctors, also had no children and died tragically."

Selma smiled.

"It's all nonsense! Besides, I just felt at home as soon as I walked in."

Over the years, she and Anton had taken in foster children at Hämma Manor. There were different reasons why the kids had nowhere else to go. Some had no parents; others had no home. Many who grew up at Hämma Manor came back years after having left to say hello, play cards, and ask for advice.

After dinner, the children cleared off the plates and fled outside. Anton went upstairs to watch *Jeopardy*. Selma and I were left alone, each with an espresso. Through the open kitchen window, we could hear the joyful sounds of the children playing. We sighed in our silence. The only sign that anyone else had been there were the stains left from the meat sauce along the long table. After a while, Selma broke the silence.

"I want to get to know you better. Tell me something."

"I've always dreamed of staying at a health resort," I said as the sky turned a pink shade of blood orange as the sun started to bow out, something it wouldn't finish until ten at night. "My grandmother once showed me a picture of big beds in high-ceilinged rooms, with staff in white aprons who brought food on a tray, and the Alps just outside the window."

"Sometimes sharing your home and your food is enough," Selma contemplated. "Full people are happy. Happy people are kind. Kind people help others."

"Giving is receiving," I summed up.

"Circle of life," she added.

* * *

Anton earned a lot in 1980s Stockholm, making a name for himself in the financial world. Selma had also done well, working in advertising. But they were restless. They wanted more. They had worked hard for years. Slowly, they had come to realize that something larger was missing from their lives. *Live Aid 1985* — when inhumane images of starving children in Ethiopia had been wired all over the world — was their wake-up call. (Alma and I had played "We Are the World" on our recorders in our nicest summer dresses outside the grocery store in Alfta — as we sold strawberry pie, juice, and our best drawings — to raise money for Save the Children.)

For Anton, that wake-up call in 1985 was one he couldn't sleep through. He felt the loss of Milo greater than ever before. Life seemed dull, and he and Selma started talking about making a change, for real. Something more than re-doing the wallpaper or going to India for six weeks of yoga.

It was around that time that he met up with an old friend from primary school. They hadn't seen each other in years and reunited over a cup of coffee at the Konditori Valand café in Stockholm's central Vasastan neighborhood. Anton asked about Märta, his friend's little sister, who had been a track and field star with the fastest time for the sixty-meter dash and long jump record holder — although Anton remembered her mostly for being so pretty. He'd had a big crush on her.

Märta was fine and working as a real estate broker up north in Leksand, where she lived with her husband, four children, three horses, three dogs, two cats, and some rabbits (it was always hard to keep track of how many there were). The family ran a bed and breakfast on Lake Siljan that allowed guests to bring their dogs and cats. It turned out to be good business.

It all sounded absolutely epic to Anton's ears. His burgeoning feelings to change his life became the focus of the conversation. There was so much to talk about that he and his friend walked from the café to the nearby Tranan restaurant to continue their discussion over dinner. Before Anton came home that night, he'd ducked into a payphone and called the unrequited love of his youth — Märta in

Leksand — who had been surprisingly receptive to the unexpected contact. What she told him was so tempting, he arranged to meet her the next day. There was no time to lose.

Selma thought he was off for a morning meeting with an American insurance company at the Grand Hôtel. Instead, Anton started his day with a coffee and cinnamon bun at a Statoil gas station and then rode up to the Dalarna province. The four-hour drive on his Harley Davidson had left him feeling freer than ever before.

* * *

The sound of Charlie Mingus's playing swung in the living room. The curtains waved at the open veranda doors as a light and lukewarm breeze came in from the Dalälven River.

With two words — "look Selma" — I let her reacquaint herself with Amelia, six years after she had bid the binder farewell. Her handwritten letter was still visible through the transparent plastic sleeve.

> *Those who are content with the world should dig into a compost heap and make themselves useful in the vegetable garden.*
>
> *Selma Björling*

She laughed so loud that Anton came down the massive stairs, in the middle of *Jeopardy*, to ask what had happened. Selma then pulled out her handwritten letter to hold it with her own hands. She had to put on her reading glasses before beginning to read it out loud.

Stockholm, May 19th, 1993

Hi Alma and Felicia,

My name is Selma Björling. I'm not related to the opera singer Jussi Björling, but I do like to sing, preferably in the shower! Do you girls also like to sing?

I live at Hämma Manor in the Dalarna province, and you are always welcome here. When I came home to our apartment one day almost ten years ago, I found rose petals in a path to the music stand my husband Anton uses when he plays the cello.

"Meet me where the stars are the closest," was written on a piece of paper attached by a clothespin.

"*Where the stars are the closest*" was the realm of Amelia Earhart, I thought to myself. Selma continued reading:

He wasn't up on our roof, which had been my first guess. I found him in the Observatorielunden park. It sits beautifully high up above the Vasastan rooftops, with stunning views of Stockholm, and even has an observatory. It's so fitting, because Anton reached up to the stars and brought them down for me, one by one.

He was lying down on a blanket, knees bent, and a hat covering his face. My husband, the love of my life, who had prepared a picnic.

"Happy birthday," he said and gave me a matchbox. It had a Dala horse on it — painted bright red with signature kurbits style decorations — the unmistakable symbol of the Dalarna province that would soon become my home.

Inside was a key. My husband had bought me a manor as a birthday gift! He's crazy!

It's a large house with lots of rooms, meadows around, close to the river where you can swim.

We want to have a huge family and would be delighted to welcome you as our guests.

Then Selma looked up again.

"We did have a huge family, just not in the way we thought," she whispered, with a hint of tears in her eyes.

"Somehow, it's better that things don't always turn out the way we thought," Anton added. "That's the charm of life that adds the magic to it."

Selma's dream of a family had come true, but only after she experienced the emotional crush of sitting opposite a doctor explaining in a friendly voice that she, unfortunately, would not be able to have children but still had many years left to live. *Dreams come true* was embroidered on the pillowcase I lay my head on at Hämma Manor. Whenever dreams changed shape, it was important to capture them. The metamorphosis from a thought to a dream and then to reality was like a caterpillar becoming a fresh and flighty butterfly.

"We got rid of the penthouse in Vasastan, the cottage right next to the ski slope in Åre, the sailboat I only took out with my guy friends," Anton said.

"...the studio apartment in southern France, your Harley Davidson, my purple Porsche," Selma continued.

"...and a dozen tailor-made Armani suits. I sold my business and promised never to waste time on another sales pitch again."

They bought books about renovating old houses, talked to some carpenters, and then they steered a rented cargo truck towards Dalarna. They felt freer than ever before, two lives on the way to new dreams — free, together.

Maybe there was a bit of truth in the nonsense warning about the manor in the village. Children weren't created at Hämma Manor, but Hämma Manor was created for children. And here Selma and Anton got the family they so desperately wanted.

"We love our life, don't we, Anton?" Selma asked.

* * *

I contacted Selma barely two months after Alma's death, on February 3rd. I had not yet become accustomed to being a singular self, after being part of a "we" that no longer existed. All that was left was just me, a self that was the loneliest self in the whole world.

During our first conversation over the phone, I could tell that Selma was made of the type of lumber that didn't grow from trees. A sacred, unique person. Before we hung up, she had invited me to her and Anton's home.

You can stay for as long as you want. We have a lot of space here, and we're used to having people around.

Then she said something that I would call to my mind again and again:

Never stop dreaming. It's your life, Felicia. You are the epicenter of your universe. For your world to be good, you must feel good. Come visit, and we can talk about dreams from morning to night.

Selma's story and the connections to and through it all were maybe more than serendipity. Why had I read about Hämma Manor in the book Dad had bought in preparation for our trip to Hälsingland last year? I called Dad to try but failed to get any answers. *Yes, Dad, I'm writing like never before. Thank you for the pen. It's worth its weight in gold.*

I went up to the room I shared with Tilda, filled to the brim with a calm that I'd been missing for a long time. Tilda was in bed with the blanket kicked off. I tucked her in before I carefully climbed up the bunk bed — wondering if the frame would hold. The joints creaked but didn't break. Postcards from Egypt, Chile, and Paris were stuck to the ceiling with thumbtacks. I pulled the curtain a little to the side of the window and saw the river behind the birch trees. A Swedish summer night in its most beautiful attire.

* * *

I woke up to a tickling sensation on the bottom of my foot. Tilda was giggling with a long blade of grass in her hand. My night had lasted forever, and I felt awake and alert. I was sure I was alive. Mellow air from the meadows had been pumped into my lungs and my eyelids were light, springing open with ease. For the first time in a long time, I felt like the old me. That day in December last year had almost killed me, but here I was, still counting sunrises.

"Come, let's go down and eat breakfast!"

I jumped down from the bunk bed and slipped into a pair of slippers Tilda had placed in a perfect position for me. They were just like the ones that had waited for me in Alma's foyer. The memories poured over me: The ringing of the bells on the coat rack whenever anyone brushed by into the apartment. Her winter outerwear hanging on the purple hooks. That ugly hat from a flea market somewhere down south. A pair of old shoes she found at the Myrorna secondhand shop. The ice-cream-cone-shaped handbag that was always slung over her shoulder so that her hair was dipped in the vanilla. Alma, my Alma, and all her ideas — now at my disposal. I lived for her idea for our adventure. Here and now. Solo, like Amelia.

* * *

The smell of summer dew sneaked through the open window. Tilda had already made her bed and told me to do the same. She pointed at a bathrobe on a hook in the wardrobe and I put it on, tying it around my waist.

"You talk a lot when you sleep. Why do you do that?"

"I do?!" I answered, surprised. "About what?"

"I can't remember everything; you really talk a lot. But you said 'Alma,' a thousand times."

"Really? I talk about Alma in my sleep?"

"What's an *Alma*?" she asked and squinted as the sunlight hit her through the window.

"Alma was my best friend."

"She's no longer your friend?" she asked in shock.

"She's still my friend, but she's no longer around. She's dead."

"My grandmother is dead. And my rabbit too."

"My grandmother is dead too. I've never had a rabbit."

"That's good. Then we really can be friends, because we know how it feels when a grandmother is dead. Maybe they met each other in heaven, your grandmother and my grandmother, and maybe my rabbit."

* * *

The kitchen table was set up like a morning buffet in an English bed and breakfast. Anton looked like a star chef with a white apron and potholders, the oven was open and he was holding a plate of bread that gave every indication, in aroma and shape, to have just been baked. On the table was a jug of *fil* — short for *filmjölk*, something like a cross between yogurt and crème fraiche that I had never come across in any other country — a large jar of orange jam, and a tin can of *müsli*, Swedish granola, with a wooden spoon in it.

Fatima, a girl I had not spoken to much, waved away a wasp with a newspaper. Juice glasses and teacups were crowded next to each other, beside a stack of bowls with spoons spread like a fan. There were tubes of *Kalles kaviar* cod roe spread, a large piece of cheese that resembled an uneven ski slope, some beekeeper's honey, apples, plums, and bananas cut in half. Oatmeal was simmering on the stove and seemed to be approaching its puffy climax. No wonder the kids loved it here. At that moment, I never wanted to leave.

My whole breakfast squeezed snugly onto a serving tray that I recognized as a Jobs Handtryck design, from the nearby village of Västanvik no doubt. I sat down on the veranda between Tilda and Fatima. Copies of the *Dagens Nyheter* and *Herald Tribune* newspapers were on the table, still unread. Current events could wait. The world could wait. I wanted to keep the new peace inside me undisturbed. These quiet moments when the soul wasn't up in arms were rare. Protected. Do not touch. Enjoy. Have breakfast and keep on smiling.

"Oh, it's all so lovely," I mumbled.

"Yes, it's really nice here. Later, let's play," Tilda said before she took a bite of her sandwich. One of the cucumber slices that lined atop the cheese slid off down onto the wooden deck.

"Ouch," she said, then picked the cucumber and quickly blew some air on it and counted 1-2-3. "That's how my dad did it before he left," she said with a shrug in response to my stare. And then she took another bite. Fatima smiled at me.

* * *

My stay at Hämma Manor had already given me a thousand years of sleep. I. Felt. Good. There was peace and quiet in the high mountains and deep valleys inside me. What had been half of *us*. But my half grew. The hours of the night had somehow multiplied. I slept better. I was tranquil. I. Was. Tranquil.

By the end of my stay, I ate enough to regain all the weight that had fallen off me after Alma's death. And my muscles for laughing, which had atrophied, were exerted in workouts that went on until I cried. The withered was being revived. A massive thundercloud had blown away from the black sky inside me. Sunbeams were finally penetrating my world of thought with rainbows from my tears of joy.

My world thawed. It was spring in my soul, and seeds gradually began to sprout after eight months of winter. Eight months of endless longing. But the magnitude of the grief never diminished. Maybe it was so that I learned to live with it. The grief was a constant weight I would carry with me forever. I grew stronger by learning to grasp it in different ways. But it never got easier. It would weigh just as much to the end of life. I got stronger, but it never got lighter.

I tried to peace myself together by returning to days of irreversible childhood and the magic of summer holidays. I played with Tilda in the woods. On warm sunny days, we went down to the river and swam. When it rained, we stayed inside, making arts and crafts, like perler bead designs. We rode bicycles and bought ice cream, laid on the grass to read, and played cards. Tilda and I invented a secret language. Quiche, fish sticks, roast beef, meatballs. Rosehip soup with almond biscuits, apple pie, family packs of hot dogs, lemonade, and cucumber water. We snacked on *filmjölk* and *smörgås* sandwiches and had strawberries with ice cream for dessert. We had a *surströmming* fermented herring party in the cabin by the water. The adults sang "Helan Går" toasting their *snaps* and the kids screamed when the opener's rusty tip penetrated the can, releasing its putrid stench.

Sun, drizzle, drizzle, sun. The river, with its leather-colored and luminous sandy bottom, was perfect for night swimming. The sweet, refreshing water, lukewarm at best, and always a degree warmer against the skin when it rained. Thunder rolled in. Four seasons in one Swedish summer day, every day.

We played games like red light, green light and *påven bannlyser* — "the pope bans" — competed in soccer and badminton tournaments, picked blueberries, and dressed up in costumes to put on skits. Under the direction of Fatima, who also wrote the script, we set up a play in the *bystuga* village hall — a local community space. An intern at the free publication *Leksandsbladet* wrote an article about the sixteen-year-old girl from Afghanistan — a talent to look out for.

What do you want to be when you grow up, Fatima?

"Become? I am already! I'm a director. I'm just going to get better at it," the girl from Kabul answers in the singsong Dalecarlian Swedish dialect.

A few days later, a reporter from the local radio station *P4 Dalarna* came out to the manor. That same evening, Fatima knocked on my door and asked if we could talk. We sat down on a blanket on the dock, and I listened to her story. Her road to Sweden.

"I miss my mother every day," she said. "I wish she could see me now. Sometimes I don't know what to do with myself. I wish it were a longing that could be filled with something else, but it will always remain."

Fatima looked out over the river. After a long silence, she said: "You've also lost someone you loved. How do you manage?"

It was still a mystery to me.

"My father gave me a pen, and I started writing. He said the words would help me find meaning in life. Fatima, with the help of words and fairy tales, you can make anything happen."

* * *

On my last day, all the children at Hämma Manor gathered on the front steps to say goodbye, like an old-fashioned family photo. Tilda jumped in next to me in the back seat and fastened her seatbelt.

"I'm coming with you," she said.

I felt a big lump in my throat. My tears flowed when I waved to all the kids running after us as we pulled away in Selma's Volvo. She put on the turn signals and honked wildly, stretched her hand out of the sunroof and waved. We went through the stately birch trees, the twelve on each side that I had counted when I rode through here for the first time. We drove out on the small forest road, crossed the bridge, and steered our way towards the station, traveling in wordless silence until we arrived.

On the platform, where the train would soon come in from Mora and continue towards Stockholm, I hugged Selma for a long time. They called out that the train was six minutes late. What luck!

"Thank you, Selma, for everything. You're an angel."

"Good people see angels. I'm proud of you. And I promise to water the forget-me-nots since it's a little dry now."

Tilda tugged on my skirt.

"I'm coming with you," she said.

I couldn't say anything. All the words were lumped together in my throat.

"Are we still best friends even though you're leaving now?"

"Best friends forever."

"But, we won't die."

"No, Tilda. We are not going to die."

I held Tilda and she shook between sobs. The damp spots her tears had left on my dress dried after my train departed from Leksand station, somewhere between Säter and Hedemora.

On the run

One step at a time, closer to the goal, I channel thoughts, run through monumental memories, make decisions. I think of early mornings when I was out exercising, the long runs around Hämma Manor and Lake Siljan, the soreness from training and the times I worried about the challenge I am taking on.

I both want to and don't want to quit the race. Tears, when I think I might make it all the way. Thinking of Alma. Alma. Alma. She is with me through several kilometers of thoughts... I have no idea how many miles...

Every now and then, I notice that I have run a long stretch without thinking at all.

All the voices, all the millions of footsteps on the pavement. The music. The train that rattles over the bridge as I run under it. The occasional siren when someone collapses and needs medical attention. I want to record my marathon, have a mini tape recorder in my pocket that picks up all the buzz and everything that is *now* as I run by. My own marathon soundtrack.

If the New York City Marathon is a Broadway musical, its most heartbreaking scene takes place on the Queensboro Bridge.

Right now.

Live.

A man in a wheelchair slowly works his way up to the highest point of the bridge. Backwards. He pushes his right foot into the asphalt and shoots up. One push, one inch closer to the goal. His marathon is a race in centimeters.

Four million of them.

Barcelona, Spain

September 1997

"I want to hear all about you and Alma," said Rosana as we sat down at her round table. "And I will tell you everything that happened to me after I passed on the binder."

At some point in our conversation, the afternoon passed on the baton of time to the evening. The dark Barcelona night picked up, and dawn finished off the relay. My handkerchief wet from my crying; we had listened to each other with a vague soundtrack reminiscent of the jazz at Hämma Manor. The *serrano* ham, tomatoes, olive oil, salt, cheeses, and a baguette had all shrunk as we spoke.

"So that's why you decided to go out and travel," Rosana said. "I would have done the same."

* * *

I had arrived in Barcelona in an E seat. As we came in for the landing, I saw the whole city below me. The plane made a turn out over the Mediterranean and then back clockwise. The force pushed me against the window. Far below me, I glimpsed rows of houses separated by streets, swimming pools, and soccer fields. Mountains in the north, and the sea's clear blue water with its shoreline. Parasols and pedal boats sprinkled the scene.

I left the baggage claim and passed through *la salida*. A couple of young policemen followed me with their eyes. The doors opened, and a Mediterranean Sea of people hung over the barrier separating those arriving and waiting. No one was here to pick me up. In a flash, I wondered: What would I feel the next time I flew back to Sweden, with no Alma waiting at arrivals? I got terrified that the loneliness would cover me up like icy lava. Alma's absence made itself known, like a scab torn off before the wound could heal.

Here and now was an inviting, continental buzz. Hollow clunks from the experienced waiters setting plates down on the airport bar's counter set the beat. I felt alive, pumped with wellbeing. I pinched my arm to capture the precious here and now that would soon wither into the there and then.

Two little sisters in cute dresses ran around and what looked like their grandparents, in matching Sunday clothes, tried to keep up. Impossible. Handsome men kissed beautiful women. Men kissed men. Women kissed women. It was a cheek kissers' paradise. Cousins, brothers, sisters, parents, and friends cried with joy when they saw their loved ones who had finally come home from studying abroad and honeymoons, with newborn babies, wives, and girlfriends.

I had either all the time in the world or maybe no time at all — depending on what the future had in store for me. I gave into fate and refused to rush. I sat down at the bar, so as not to miss this spectacle — because that's what Barcelona Airport was — and I had a front-row seat. A 007-type of a man, stunning in a dark suit with a copy of *El País* under his arm, sat down at the vacant barstool next to me. He looked around and ordered *un café solo* — smiled at me — and raised his eyebrows as he downed his coffee, before a young girl, his daughter, ran up to him. Two generations were reunited and he kissed her on the cheek. I thought of Dad. Was he sitting in his favorite spot in the library? Had he turned the book over, leaving it open cover up, and gone for an espresso?

A sense of gratitude — an urge to thank him — suddenly overwhelmed me! Dad had convinced me that "the helpers" would find me. He had given me the gift of confidence, and I had applied it to the twenty-seven letters of the alphabet. To the periods, semicolons, and ampersands. My diary had always traveled with me no matter what. Without it, I felt… alone. If I didn't write for a few days, I would feel something inside me rumbling at low frequency. An earthquake, a natural disaster that could only be prevented with my own words, written in one notebook after another. They were all different. All of their unruled pages had been filled. All were lined up from the first to the 122nd in my room in London. The travel journal where I was telling the story now would join them after this trip. The 123rd. Its black elastic band around the covers was already beginning to stretch. I was filling the pages with ordinary words strung together and transformed into something more, with and to my heart's content.

After I finished my coffee, I made my way to the exit. Another gateway. The heat smacked into me as I left the air-conditioned arrivals area. A sense of familiarity hit me before my sandals slapped on the hot asphalt. I felt like a returnee even though I had never been here before. *Mi casa es tu casa*, Barcelona whispered in my ear. I took in the palm trees, yellow-black taxis, and all the tourists. I was an adventurer and explorer following in the footsteps of the binder. I was the Amelia we had set out to be.

The airport bus to the main square of Plaça Catalunya ran along a motorway that cut through sparse countryside lined with mountains on the outskirts of the city. The traffic became heavier and slower the closer we got to the city center. Guys drove mopeds with girls on the back, tanned legs and hands around six-packs. I watched a cloud of pigeons sweep in and take a seat next to a fountain where a man was selling helium balloons that were like an upturned bunch of grapes. Balloons, like the ones Alma had brought with her when she picked me up at Arlanda airport almost nine months ago.

September had just knocked on the calendar door, but the day was still hot. I walked down Portal de l'Àngel towards the sea. I passed one shoe store after another, each doorway offering a few seconds of cooling scented by cheap potpourri that tickled my nose. I glimpsed a giant neon thermometer far up along a building's facade. Its "mercury" was up to 29 °C. A street musician played guitar, a clown juggled, and a group of dancers was trying to animate the audience as they sent a hat around to fill up with *pesetas*. I watched for a while, looking around in 3D. My senses went *File, New, and Save as*, archiving impressions in a folder with the working title *Amelia*.

I turned around and let my eyes float up to the wooded mountains far above the city. A thin border of green separated the metropolis and the sky. My eyes fixed on a large house with a roof like a slanted hat. The contours were sharp as razor blades cutting into the clear blue sky. I continued in the direction of the Mediterranean but could not let go of the house on the mountain. An American family asked me about the Els Quatre Gats café, a hangout for Picasso and his paintings in the 1890s. I laughed — I was a backpacker new in town! They instead turned to a woman who pointed to the left, and the family turned into an alley. The majestic Catedral de Barcelona, with its grand towers reaching for the sky, popped into my view as I took a left after a Picasso mural. Couples were sitting on the cathedral stairs kissing and a woman with long braids tried to sell them AIDS pins — red ribbons folded in half with a safety pin straight through.

An elderly man in a gray beard sat resting in the shade with his socks off, drying away in the sun. I imagined he was the architect Antoni Gaudí. I'd read about him. He was fatally struck by a tram while walking from the La Sagrada Familia construction site in the summer of 1926. He had been so dirty and shabby looking that no one recognized him. So insignificant that no one bothered to immediately help him, and when they did, he was taken to a hospital for the poor. Only later did they realize that it was the master-builder himself who had been injured.

Did Alma see her life play out like a movie when she got hit by the car? Had it ended with *The End*? Or if there was an afterlife, *To be continued...*

And what about we, who survived, who were not snatched away forever, who were not buried. We, who did not die, every day. We who collected a little more footage before our film's morbid premiere for its solo spectator.

Why Alma and why Gaudí? Two lives, with a definite beginning and end, and the in-between that would live in the stories told by others. When Gaudí died, the zealots took over. They archived his drawings, built on his projects, and wrote about him in textbooks. That's how history is shaped by the storytellers. And it was me championing for Alma now, trying to ensure her short life story was not in vain. Thanks to a bearded old man placed along my path in the shade, Gaudí became another brick in my mourning walk.

I soon crossed Via Laietana, leaving the mythical Barri Gòtic — the gothic quarters — behind. My eyes were set on the La Ribera neighborhood and its crown jewel church. The ambiance here was worn, but something was growing that refined the roughness, a neighborhood on the verge of becoming popular and expensive. I walked through stenches of urine and marijuana. A lady was closing before *la siesta* and pulled her store's shutters down with a rattling thunder. A group of tourists probably heading to the Picasso museum took a small, side street. I walked in total bliss, playing a mental game of counting all the good-looking people I saw along the way with a double jackpot if two were holding hands. The score was soon in the hundreds.

When I made it to the church of Santa Maria del Mar, built in just fifty-five years — or three of Alma's lifetimes — in the 14th century, I just had to trudge across the adjacent square to get to Rosana's apartment. A bride, cigarette in hand, waited on the church steps. At Plaça de Santa Maria 4, I buzzed for the third-floor apartment.

"*Sí?*" called a woman in an ascending scale.

"*Hola, soy Felicia,*" I said.

"Felicia! *Pasa pasa!*" — and then the apparatus crackled and beeped, signaling that the door was open.

The stairs up were narrow and windy and went counterclockwise. I held myself against the cold railing. TVs were on, a smoky voice shouted at Josep Maria, and a phone rang without anyone answering. The door to Rosana's apartment was open when I got there.

"Felicia! I can't believe you're here!" Rosana cried as she embraced me. I got two big kisses on the cheeks, and before I had time to say anything more than "Hello, it's nice to see you, I mean meet you for the first time," she had said pretty much the same thing and much, much more.

The balcony doors were open, with the city floating in as casually as if it was a roommate. It was a perfect little apartment with beams in the ceiling and a small guest room facing the courtyard where I would stay, next to her daughter Isabella's room. The walls were covered with pictures of mother and daughter. Moments from the beach, on horseback, on a walk in the woods. Isabella was at her grandmother's house in Òdena — an hour outside Barcelona — spending the last bit of her holiday playing with all the horses, dogs, and cats together with her cousins and neighbors' kids. A playful summer. I felt a lightning hit of nostalgia deep in my chest, reminiscing. Tilda had brought it out, so I knew for sure that I still had that child within.

Rosana had made a bed for me in the sparsely decorated guest room. It was like a blank canvas, with a white crocheted bedspread, a ceiling lamp with a shade made of cream-colored embroidered cloth, and a Joan Miró poster on the wall. The wooden floor sloped slightly and was made of wide planks. The window was open and I could see a neighbor's briefs, jeans, and shirts hanging to dry across the inner courtyard. Off to the side, a few flats away, a young woman, tan with hair down to her waist, was watering some red geraniums. She waved, I smiled. She nodded, I blushed. After unpacking my backpack and putting all my belongings in the drawers, I went back to the kitchen. It was a Tuesday with a scent of coffee.

"Now Felicia, I want to hear everything," said Rosana, passing me a cup. It was that prompt that kicked off hours of conversation.

"We made a promise — a pinky swear — to make this journey together. But then Alma died. I tried contacting everyone who put something in the binder. I'm visiting five of you, Amelia's angels."

Rosana looked into my eyes for a long time.

"I like that, Felicia," she said and smiled. "A sisterhood of solo pilots reaching for nothing but the sky together."

"Wait a minute, I'm going to get something," I said and went into my room.

The binder was in my backpack, still wrapped in the same cloth bag it had been sent back in. My travel companion and co-pilot, Amelia.

"Look, Rosana..."

"...*madre mia*," she whispered. "*Madre mia.*"

Rosana held the binder in her hands. Amelia, who had helped Rosana's dreams take off. Her gaze went out to the rooftops. I put my hand on her shoulder and said good night. It was half-past two when I lay down with the city life still awake outside my open window. The clock read 04:56 AM when I opened my eyes again. Bakery smells were rising from below. I heard high-heeled footsteps and small talk going down the street. A moped passed by, then a garbage truck. The buzzing neighborhood was a stark contrast to the nightly stillness of Hämma Manor. I had hopscotched between welcoming worlds, and with that, I closed my eyes again.

A paper bag of croissants and a glass of freshly squeezed orange juice were waiting for me on the kitchen table when I got up a few hours later. An upturned plate protected the juice from flies. I turned on the radio, and the voices of two debating women filled the room. The neighbors' TV was on, and a waiter in the square was setting up chairs and tables. Mopeds flew through the *plaça*. The pigeons spread their wide wings and fluttered up to the rooftops.

Rosana and I were already friends for life after the first night, as if that day hadn't been the first time we'd met. I guessed she was about thirty-five years old. She'd seen twice as many sunrises as I had.

"I want to show you what the binder left in its wake, but first I'll prepare some *bocadillos*," Rosana said, referring to what I later learned were baguettes with *jamón serrano* ham, omelet-like *tortilla de patatas* made from potatoes and egg, a thin layer of tomato, garlic, salt, and olive oil.

* * *

Six years ago, Amelia had added Rosana to her flight path. Rosana Mundi was sitting in a café in Barcelona. Next to her *café con leche*, lay the binder. She was studying architecture at Universitat Politecnica de Catalunya and wrote *JUST DO IT, ROSANA* in red marker on a page of her dissertation, folded it, and put it in the binder. She was waiting for a friend who was about to go on holiday to the Easter Islands off Chile. He was late. To kill time, Rosana went for a walk and saw a notice on a bulletin board.

A nearby company was hiring people for a new renovation project: a restaurant converted from a market in *El Born*, the neighborhood in between Via Laietana and Barceloneta, known for its narrow medieval streets. Everything just fell into place. There and then. Rosana felt she'd found her calling, and then her friend showed up. When they said goodbye the next morning, he had the binder with him in his suitcase. Rosana had the job notice, and she was soon asked to come in for an interview.

It was 1992, and *two* dreams were growing within Rosana. A pregnancy test that would soon lay on the bathroom counter, smiling up at her with its positivity. Rosana hopped in her red Volkswagen Beetle convertible — bearing its many scratches from years of tight, curbside parking on the Barcelona streets — and drove to the bar where she'd been working for the past three years. She resigned. Without hesitation, she then drove on to her second job at a dry cleaner and greeted her boss with the announcement that she was sick and tired of ironing shirts and would never be coming back. Then she drove to the company that was looking for people for the restaurant renovation project.

"I had nothing to lose. I gave it my all and got the job."

The concept at *El Mercat* — the market — was simple. Diners chose from the vegetables of the day, and the chef quickly whipped up a soup, served with a piece of bread and water. *El Mercat* was a steep learning curve with a tasty ending. Through word of mouth, Rosana's name started traveling around town. She renovated stores, restaurants, and boutique hotels, but wanted more control and decided to go solo. Or *sola*, as Rosana thought of it. Two years after *El Mercat,* she set up her own firm. Her manifesto was to always 1) maintain the authenticity of the city; 2) use only sustainable materials; and 3) hire talent born and bred in Barcelona.

Rosana's life had taken a new turn thanks to the direct message of encouragement she had written to herself and left in the binder. *JUST DO IT, ROSANA.*

* * *

"The place I want to take you today was built in 1925, and we're turning it into a hotel. A lot has happened there over the years. For a while, it was a hospital. *Vamos!*"

I got ready and wondered what kind of house we were going to visit. I loved old houses, as did Selma and Anton. And Rosana. Was that another common factor that all of us in the binder shared? Aside from flying high and wanting to leave our mark on the world, did we also fall for abandoned houses?

With our sights set on the mountain of Tibidabo, we left the medieval area of La Ribera behind and drove through the city's distinctly different neighborhoods. Into the picture-perfect Eixample, with its corners chopped off — creating views of hollow octagons from above — we rode, then along the Avinguda Diagonal, as it cut up blocks into new shapes. I rolled down the window to inhale the bohemian vibe of the free-spirited Gràcia. More air and green appeared between the buildings as the residential Sant Gervasi, Les Tres Torres, and Sarrià followed suit. The latter was where wealthy Barcelona residents had traveled by horse and carriage in the early 20th century to enjoy the summers away from the hustle and bustle.

We turned onto a sloping street that soon wound its way up through Barcelona's shy mountains like a Swiss serpentine road. I felt so special sitting in the passenger seat, with the binoculars hanging around my neck. No one else in the world was sitting where I was now. I could see the whole city on my side while Rosana's view was blocked by the rising mountain walls outside her window.

I imagined flying like a bird to the 1992 Olympic Stadium at the mountain of Montjuïc — right across town — then flapping my wings on to the pinnacles and towers of La Sagrada Familia, and then dipping my feet on the shores of the Mediterranean to taste the saltiness at the water's edge. Then I was taking off again. Solo, Amelia, me. What views from above! Buildings standing strong, conversing with each other. I looped around between them and chirped *buenas tardes*. Old, worn, and modern houses with plenty of stories absorbed by their walls or let out through open summer windows. I flew free and crazy, happy, and limitless. I had spread my wings! I was alive!

Rosana's voice pulled me out of my fantasy flying:

"We're coming up on it now. Just a few more turns and we're there."

A long string of cyclists — like links in a chain — whizzed past on the curvy way down to the city.

"Rosana, you didn't say it was practically a castle!"

* * *

Atanasio, the caretaker, came out carrying a bucket. He waved and let us in through the gate, which connected to the high fence like the clasp on a necklace. Rosana parked next to Atanasio's moped and locked the radio in the glove compartment. The road curved around the house and the greenery did a fine job concealing the first floor. Its milky façade stretched six floors above the treetops. Judging by the bushy hedges, the garden would need a lot of attention in the future. I looked up at the sky and was dazzled by the sun.

"They start work in a couple of weeks," Atanasio said. "You're lucky to see it before the transformation."

Creeping vines of woodbine ruled green supreme along the facade. Atanasio showed us in — it was an astonishing piece of architecture. Velvet curtains from the ceiling touched the parquet floor. The windows were nailed shut with plywood boards, but sunlight still crept in through the cracks. It drew long stripes on the wooden floor and crooked into the dents left from dancing high-heeled shoes. The hinges on the tall glass doors creaked as we walked through into an immense ballroom on the other side.

An old bar, where plenty of drinks had been served, stretched along the wall. Ernest Hemingway, Pablo Picasso, and Salvador Dalí used to come here and hobnob with lady companions who filled out their dresses until their full breasts seemed almost ready to spill over like the drinks being poured. They drank cloudy absinthe — wormwood liqueur — and smoked pipes while the cabaret dancers changed before the second act in the small theater hall next door.

"Isn't this absolutely amazing?" Rosana said. "I'm so glad you can see it before we start the renovation work! I wonder how much of this wouldn't have happened if I hadn't met that Greek lady at the art exhibition, who gave me your binder."

The tree branches outside moved in the arhythmic and wild wind. An elevator gaped empty next to a wooden staircase that coiled up through the house. It looked like it had been struck dead in the middle of a yawn. Who was the last to press its buttons? We went up the stairs, one floor at a time. There were room numbers left on some doors on the third floor.

"Who stayed in here?" I wondered aloud, then knocked on the door to room 67. I called "Room service" as I entered.

The room was empty except for a dresser with a mirror, sitting alone on the floor, as if seeking company. On the back of an old passport photo I had in my wallet, I wrote *Felicia Fanny Äng was here* and placed it in the attached mirror stand's tiny drawer. I closed the door behind me and continued to explore. Rosana ran down to help Atanasio with a delivery of kitchen tiles from a supplier in downtown Eixample. The floors became brighter the higher up I climbed the stairs. Closer to heaven, no one had nailed the windows shut. When I reached the top — the sixth floor — I explored every nook until I found a door that led out onto a roof terrace with a massive panoramic view. I found a piece of wood and stuck it in the door so I wouldn't get locked out.

Barcelona lay safely protected between the sea and mountains. I felt guarded too. I wanted this happiness, warm in my soul like a buzzing bumblebee, to stay with me for a while longer. Here and now, like there and then, all my senses were activated. The ones I had left behind to survive and the ones that had faded. The screams from nearby amusement park carousels became my pacemaker. Angry dogs at neighboring houses gave me my hearing back. The smell of the wind, the gnarled wall where my hand lay and felt the history of the house's walls. I was waking up from a slumber that had held me captive since December 22nd last year.

I had come down for a landing at *Felicia Fanny Äng Airport* and caught up with myself on a rooftop in Barcelona. From what I could remember, my soul and I met the last time no later than the second before learning of Alma's death. Since then, they had stayed far apart, uninterested in reuniting. It was forever and ever ago. Another time, another me. Before life had turned me into a solo performance.

Up above the Atlantic

October 1997

I didn't open the letter from Rosana until the plane reached cruising altitude. I wanted to savor any upcoming emotions when I could. My journey towards my own discoveries continued as I sailed on, high up in the blue with the sea far below me.

"*Te quiero volver a ver,*" Rosana had said to me at Plaça Catalunya as the airport bus approached.

My heart had raced, and I had put my backpack down on the Catalan tiles and quickly ran across the *plaça* to get her a helium balloon. I shouted, "Thank you, Barcelona!" with my arms in the air as I ran back just in time for the bus to depart.

"I am sure we will meet again," I whispered. "This is not our last hug. I will be back."

* * *

I dozed off, immersed in deep-sea dreams. Flying over an ocean's depth of water, my body jerked, and I opened my eyes. We had moved a few more kilometers westward. Below me thousands of meters of air, and then a mass of water like no other. I just could not get my mind around how the universe functioned. For thousands of years, only birds could fly, but then one day, we humans took off too, and then a yellow dot we called the moon became accessible.

And — why did Alma die? There we were again. The question mark hung in my mind's eye. Bold font, *Times New Roman*, size 96. It scared the living hell out of me that I might never erase the question mark and turn what was being asked into a statement. Get rid of the crap at the top so that only the dot at the bottom remained. Add a few more lines afterwards that would fully answer my queries. Of all the things I yet had to comprehend, Alma's sudden death was the most incomprehensible. I twisted and turned in vain, and she would always be gone.

Only memories remained. Forget-me-not, tell me, when are you going to bloom on the mountain of Tibidabo? Will you befriend the grapevine growing on the wall behind you?

The sea under the cloud cover separated the past in Barcelona and the present that awaited me at the plane's destination. I sailed on in a blue sky until, finally, we made the descent for a landing. Amelia Earhart's home ground.

It never gets easier

I bounce past runners as if I had super springs in the soles of my shoes. There are thoughts of friends going online, following my race step by step. In real-time, they can see me pass 5 km, 10, 15, in New York. I run down city block after city block — sometimes through the lukewarm stench from the Porta Potties where boys pee quickly and girls stand in line. Exactly the same smell all over the world. Roll my sleeves up, check my watch every five kilometers and notice that my daydreams of cake are still going strong. Here, I burn calories.

I finally arrive in Manhattan. A sharp turn, and I reach the dreaded First Avenue — a hundred blocks of hell in an infinitely long and straight line. With legs heavy as bowling balls, I head north. They carry me, but I wonder how. A wide field of heads bounce on in front of me. First Avenue, the endless First Avenue. Right foot, left foot; right, left; right, left. This endless foolish clomping and stomping. Right foot, left foot; right, left; right, left. This endless foolish clomping stomping. Right... Yes, I am doing the right thing.

How many blocks left to go? Thirty? Forty? Eighty?

I'm glad that my shoelaces don't come untied. And no pebbles are in my shoes.

The sign for the 27 km mark may as well say *Hell*. Can I order some new legs at The Body Shop? How long would I have to wait?

I want to throw up. Clamp my jaw shut. Stop and quit. Keep going and finish. All these incurable contrasts spin in my head. I really think for a while that this is not possible and that I need to quit. But then I manage to pass 30 km. 18 miles. Thirty thousand meters. I have never run farther than this before. Now I'm out on new ground. Exploring. The head believes that the body is doing ok. It's still hard, but it can't get worse than this.

New York City, USA

Mrs. Hewson was a very elegant lady. Her wardrobe was filled to the brim with fine clothes that she selected with care every night and hung on a door hook before going to bed. There was always a new necklace around her neck. She let the curlers sit in during breakfast, covered by a floral shawl she tied at the back of her neck. Once a month, she went and got her nails done. Her wedding ring shone, like the liveliness in her eyes. She was in love with life and the life she had. At the age of twenty-five, she had moved to Africa. Now Mrs. Hewson lived alone in an apartment on Spring Street in Manhattan.

* * *

The journey from JFK airport first took me to Grand Central. I stopped for a moment on the main concourse and gazed up at its celestial sphere. A little girl lost her grip on the string of her balloon and began to cry inconsolably. The balloon sailed up, slowly but surely, waddling like a slow tango. It soon found peace in the starry sky, handled with care by Alma. I sucked the moment into a mental pipette that dumped it wherever in the brain vivid memories are stored.

An hour later, on Spring Street, I took out my travel journal and started looking for Mrs. Hewson's exact address. A man offered to help me.

"I'm on my way to my friend Mrs. Hewson. I have her address here…" I began.

"Felicia, what a coincidence," he said, holding out his hand and introducing himself as Victor Hewson, Mrs. Hewson's son. A handsome man in his fifties, a bit of a dandy with a masculine scent and a deeply melodic voice. My cheeks must have turned red — I could feel the blush! — and I couldn't think of anything to say. It was as if I had met a decade younger Morgan Freeman. Victor offered to carry my bag and I let go without hesitation.

"Come on, let's go home. Mother lives close by."

We walked to an apartment building a couple of blocks away. I followed him up the winding stairs to the second floor.

"Happy birthday, Mother!" Victor shouted through the door. "I have a present for you! And not just the usual bouquet of tulips I give you every year."

I teared up a bit when Mrs. Hewson came forward to greet me, limping slightly with a walking stick in her hand. I heard a commotion inside the apartment. They were having a party. She was the birthday girl, stunning in her party dress and a silver barrette holding back her curly ash-gray hair. She put her hands on my shoulders and looked at me for what seemed like a long time — she buzzed with history and experience. My gaze focused into her eyes, which had seen so much of the world. This woman had lived a life, a long life, and one that was unlike any other.

"Felicia, I can't believe you're here. What a birthday gift!" she said, motioning me toward my room. "You can stay as long as you want! Felicity is in India and won't be back until spring, so you can sleep in here!"

"Thanks so much. I may just move in!"

"Be my guest darling," Mrs. Hewson laughed.

* * *

I had stepped into a living home, celebrating Mrs. Hewson with champagne and almond cake. The bouquets of flowers were plentiful and generous. Cards and letters from near and far were lined up on a table. Mrs. Hewson seemed to have many friends. I had barely set my backpack in my room before she grabbed my hand and introduced me to all the party guests. There were almost sixty! They were a lovely random mix of widows, librarians, and professors; botanists, writers and diplomats; artists, musicians, and poets. This was how I wanted to age too, among good friends.

My stay in New York began festively with an eightieth birthday, enveloped in sacred friendship. Every day afterwards I would find traces of confetti left in the apartment. Two weeks later, I ran a marathon for the first time in my life. The race helped heal the broken me. Every day I enjoyed many rewarding conversations with Mrs. Hewson. She was intelligent and well-read. And what a sense of humor! Sometimes she acted out Monty Python scenes that had me bent over laughing! It seemed that all that happiness trapped inside me had finally been released. And it felt great. Victor visited his mother a few times a week, adding luster to our worldly conversations.

"I think I've read almost three thousand books, on just about any subject matter," Mrs. Hewson said during one of our talks. "About a year ago, I was into Japanese architecture and read everything I could find about it."

"No wonder I became a journalist. Mom read and Dad wrote," Victor said. "There were words everywhere. Do you write Felicia?"

"Yes, every day."

"My father kept a diary all his life. He started when he was nine and kept on until he couldn't hold a pen anymore."

"When Nelson was very ill, with death closing in, he asked me to read aloud from his diaries. I had never thought of asking to read them before," Mrs. Hewson said and smiled at me. "A part of life is just for ourselves. We all have secrets that are our own."

I couldn't have agreed more. For me, journal entries were personal and sometimes a naked, almost raw, depiction of a double life no one knew about. Truths only the writer and the ink were witnesses to.

"Mother, please tell Felicia about the diaries."

Mrs. Hewson closed her eyes, and through a deep breath, she returned to a time when there were no more dawns in store for her husband. Soon he would be gone forever.

With a thin, barely audible whisper, Nelson had asked his beloved wife to go into the library next door and pick up Diary 1. It was at the top of the shelf, at the far left. Mrs. Hewson had to use the ladder and trembled a little on her hand as she gently pulled out a small piece of history, dusting it off with a handkerchief before returning to the room where Nelson would soon be no more.

In the light of three candles on the table next to the edge of the bed, she started reading aloud to Nelson. His own words, as he'd written them sixty years ago. All those pages. A whole life in words. Immortalized letters that deciphered joy, hope, and faith in the future. Ugly doodles that indicated an imbalance in body and soul.

"His first ever journal entry was on May 5th, 1934. Nelson and his brother Paul played in the river, and their Uncle Christopher taught them carpentry. Nelson was barely conscious, but when I read to him, I knew he could hear."

Nelson had written in great detail about his first trip to Chicago, sitting in the front seat next to his Dad the whole way. The thrill of traveling from one place together — collecting Americana on the way — planted dreams to explore the big wide open and lands beyond. Towards the irrevocable end, Nelson became calmer and calmer as each passing moment added to the story. His breaths became shallower, but he persevered, as if waiting for something. He held onto life and Mrs. Hewson continued to read. There were not many words left between them now. In hopes of getting a few more minutes together, she slowed down.

Finally, Mrs. Hewson turned the page for Nelson's detailed description of returning home, spotting the house's roof from afar. His father at the wheel, window open. Nelson next to him. Gifts for the other kids hidden in the trunk. The joy that elated him at the thought of finally telling his little brother Paul about the journey and all its adventures. Mrs. Hewson heard the hint of a whisper and put her ear close to her husband's mouth.

"I am home, my love. Please come visit."

* * *

Everything was quiet my last night before leaving. The dresser drawers, hollow after I'd taken out my clothes, mirrored the sensation of my heart. Wardrobe hangers moved slightly until they regained their balance. I was already missing the rose-scented hand soap that was so thoughtfully placed in my bathroom — and the artifacts from countries the Hewson family had traveled to: A deep purple bedspread from India with matching pillows from Felicity in New Delhi, the Lladro figurines on the bedside table, and the giraffes with their long necks in the bookshelf next to books about Nelson Mandela, Martin Luther King, Jr., and Nina Simone. But what I would miss the most were the fresh flowers on my bedside table, replaced with love several times during my stay.

I opened my travel journal and flipped back to the first sentence I had written in New York. I had expected some kind of answer on how to move on with life. And then it hit me — it was not about me moving on, it was about the world moving me.

On the way to the kitchen to get a glass of water, I saw a streak of light fluttering joyfully through the doorway into the studio. I peeked in quietly. Candles, uneven in length, sat lit in wine bottles along the windowsill. Their light reflected in the window dark with night. A teacup next to the tulips bore dark red lipstick marks around the edge. Mrs. Hewson stood at an easel, her paintbrush caressing the canvas. She had barred art altogether during Nelson's illness, afraid it would eat up the limited time left together. With the passage of time, she had eventually made the crossing into a new mental space and now surrounded herself with all the color she allowed back into her lonely heart.

The first morning when her world no longer had Nelson in it, she had crossed the studio threshold and grabbed her watercolors. Inspired by his last words, she let herself become one with art. Her piece — which she had titled *Home* — had then traveled around the world with Amelia the binder, eventually arriving in Sweden. From there, it was safely stored in a backpack carried firmly on my shoulders as I made my great journey. After resting in drawers at Hämma Manor and in Barcelona, *Home* had been reunited with Mrs. Hewson a decade after she painted it.

Home sweet home.

Why continue?

So why do I do it?

Why do I keep running?

It really is like hell, honestly. I curse the "little enemies" who settle into my head and try to convince me to stop running even though I won't. I thank Alma for sending me out on this journey — with its interconnected moments of joyful joy and slips on banana peels. It's Alma, who ultimately got me to the starting line. It's not easy to get there, whatever the race.

I'm crossing Willis Bridge. These bridges, where the steps become shorter and shorter in sluggish uphills. It is so tough on the thighs. It hurts so much.

What am I doing?

Finally, entering the Bronx, bye Manhattan. Madison Avenue Bridge. Another bridge. My poor thighs. And somewhere up above — Alma

Sunday lounging with her legs up and a cappuccino — a perfect helicopter view of my suffering. But she knows it will get me places.

Havana, Cuba

November 1997

To deceive American authorities a bit, I stopped over in Mexico City — which included a mesmerizing visit to Frida Kahlo's Blue House — before making my way to my next destination. Soon a sea of islands was below me. My stomach tingled with increasing intensity when I glimpsed the tropics thousands of meters below. I sat, like a child on her first flight, and stared out the window, snapping Kodak moments. Everything was blue or green. I was on my way to Cuba in Hemingway's footsteps.

The plane landed comfortably at José Martí International Airport, and we deboarded. The é in the main sign's *José* had fallen off and no one had bothered to hang it back up. It was like a musical note that had escaped in the middle of a crescendo. The woman who checked my passport had short black hair, an *Hasta la victoria siempre* pin on her chest, and a baton hanging on the hip. She collected my tourist visa — the passport-sized paper that had been processed at the Cuban embassy in London — and I entered the country without the slightest trace in my passport.

I got into a taxi with a peeling Chevrolet sticker that had started to curl up at the edges in its rear windshield. I thought of Alma picking me up at Arlanda and how we had stuffed my bag in with all the things she had forgotten to take out. How I had sat in the passenger seat next to her, wrapped in a picnic blanket and feeling that I had landed in Sweden only when I recognized the license plates on the other cars. Three letters, three digits — just like here in Cuba. On the bright yellow background of a passing car's license plate, I read HDW 413 — capitalized and bold — and felt that exact sensation of having landed in a new country.

The palm trees were bowed along the roadside as if to greet me on my maiden voyage to the hotel in Havana where I'd booked a few nights. In five weeks, I would be on my next round of international flights for the last leg of this journey. Havana — Mexico City — Toronto — Osaka.

Did I long for home? Not one bit. It housed all the memories of Alma. She was everywhere there. Her presence — lack of presence, or maybe absence? — was less tangible on the road. I could escape. But like most journeys, mine was to be capped with an inescapable return. The unpacking of bags, the revealing of luggage. Some of it hopefully lost on the way. About two months from now, at the end of January next year — 1998 already, time flies — I would board a British Airways flight from Osaka. My mother and father would pick me up at Heathrow for *The End*, probably without helium balloons.

* * *

Rhythms sprinkled through open windows and balcony doors, making my feet tap new beats and hips swing a little more than usual. People moved in symbiosis with music that filled every nook and corner of Havana. The feeling that I had been here before grabbed hold of me. A reunion or my first time visiting? A welcome? The sky peaked down through occasional rows of glassless windows, revealing that some buildings were just facades with nothing behind them. Maybe one day, an architect like Rosana would roll up her sleeves, give it a roof, fill in the empty interior, and make it a home sweet home.

Hotel Gran Louisa was located in Habana Vieja. A brochure next to the cash register at the reception explained that the celebrated painter Louisa del Bosque had lived here in the 1880s. I read about a vase with a cherry blossom design acquired during one of her trips to the Far East. It now rested on a shelf in the lobby — sunflowers in it — right next to where breakfast was served each morning. I went up to the roof terrace for a cup of coffee while waiting for my room to be ready. The setting sun hovered just above a blue strip of sea. It was finishing up its day of fading the already washed-out pastel-painted beachfront buildings as they faced the waves. The rays warmed my shoulders, and I sank into the present moment.

I was spending a few days in Havana before my trip east to Santiago de Cuba. Clara Santos was waiting for me at her *casa particular* — an accommodation for tourists who prefer a home over a hotel. More than once, I got lost in Havana's constant current of color. Its eye-catching laundry hung over me as I walked down alleys and listened to the rattling ring of telephones from open windows. The everyday sounds of Cuba exposed themselves in full nudity. I took photos, went to museums, and rolled cigars — moving my mind's material to a travel journal meant for two. Pages meant for shared memories were just my memories now.

The men of the city smiled and followed me with their eyes as I walked the streets in my sandals. They whistled to get my attention — and my wallet out — for sunflowers, cigars, and black-and-white postcards of Che Guevara. One day, my footsteps took me to *Amistad* street. The name was Spanish for friendship. I used to think *"amistad"* always lasted forever. But nothing is forever and "always" has no guarantees. "Always" was a lie.

* * *

I put off the one thing I had to do in Havana until my last night. In our joint travel journal, Alma wrote down the restaurant La Guarida. She had seen a documentary on SVT about the restaurant's restoration work before its opening in July last year — just a few months before the binder came back to us. Alma had dreamed of eating there, and a few days later, she was gone. I felt obligated to go, but even as I made my way there from the hotel, I still didn't know if I could go through with it.

How do you get a table for one that should have been a table for two? Act when your loneliness is so brutally exposed? When you just want to roar out your grief and turn off the light?...

The stairs up to the restaurant entrance didn't make it easier. The marble staircase curled counterclockwise from the ground floor. I grabbed hold of the handrail and began my ascent along an outer wall with paint that was flaking. I took one step at a time, resting on each foot. There was no desire to go forward. I wanted to put off the inevitable for a few more seconds. A hostess led me to a table set for a single person with a rose in a small vase as the finishing touch. The empty chair sitting opposite me was as hollow as my heart. Wherever my gaze drifted, it returned to the emptiness on the other side. My best friend should have been sitting there, smiling and laughing.

How do you fill the silence when you are alone? Make time go by when it has stopped in the dark? Is there an escape from one's thoughts? Maybe like Fatima — the young theater director at Hämma Manor — we had to invent stories to escape. I took out the travel journal and started writing. My eyes fixed on a photograph of Ernest Hemingway with his pipe in his mouth. The pen gained momentum in my hand.

> *Mr. Hemingway, do you remember the stately Gran Hotel La Florida, perched high on the prosperous hills of Barcelona?*

> *It was built by a Catalan man, Doctor Andreu, in 1924, and used as a hospital during the Spanish Civil War 1936 to 1939. Later on, in the 1950s, it turned into a summer getaway for the upper class.*

> *Say, Mr. Hemingway, do you remember your stay there?*

> I'm sure I saw him nod.

> *Isn't it funny that you and I spent time in the same room, walked on the same floor, and breathed under the same roof?*

> *Did you see theater performances there? Go to masquerades? Hang out at the bar well into the wee hours?*

I turned my gaze back to the half-profile photograph.

When I close my eyes, I envision you there. An army of writers.

Did you sit in the cool of the twilight heat on the roof with a daiquiri, looking out over the city?

Or down outside the main entrance, facing the mountains?

Did you write there?

Words grown out of nothing, into ink on paper and then into books.

I am sure he said "*Sí sí, señorita*" with a tiny accent.

Are there any words left for me too? What would you say, Mr. Hemingway?

Or have all the words and stories already been captured and told?

I put down my pen and felt completely numb. My hand was damp. Soon a calm matured within me; I felt at home and no longer as lonely. La Guarida had enriched me. I thanked Alma for the restaurant recommendation and paid. A Polaroid picture from Brooklyn fell out of the travel journal when I got up to leave. Victor had named the photo *An infinite second* and looked me so deep in the eye with his Morgan Freeman gaze that I barely knew where to go. And then he had said: "*You have a whole world of words in you. Write.*"

I walked back in the Havana dark, on gnarled asphalt, and passed open windows where music flowed out unhindered. A car drove past me, the driver honked and waved. I felt a halving heartache from knowing I would leave the very next day, but also complete after visiting La Guarida. I ended my stay in Havana at the same place where it started: on the hotel's roof terrace where the starry Cuban night seemed so full of possibilities — if I only dared to reach for them. I dried my tears of joy with my father's handkerchief. The little soft piece of cloth had been through so much.

Sunbeams and the bright colors of palm trees clung shamelessly to the Aero Caribbean's fuselage as I took off for Santiago de Cuba the next morning. My seat assignment, *16A*, was handwritten on my boarding pass in blue ink. The engines started up, and just as the guidebook said, they served soft drinks, rum, and nuts.

The man in the seat next to me was on his way home from visiting his sick sister. He introduced himself as Jose Saroza. There was something about the sound of his last name that made me accept when he offered a ride from the airport into the city.

"How can I pay you?"

"I was going this way anyway. Just tell me a little about yourself."

* * *

I was traveling the path of Amelia the binder and was going to meet Clara, a seamstress in Vista Alegre in Santiago de Cuba. Alma and I were childhood friends who had played together when we were little and even when we got older.

We climbed trees, swam, and drew treasure maps. I told him about our summers. The view up on the roof to see the world from a different angle. I described the forests, the lakes, and the water lilies. Every Midsummer's Eve, I picked seven flowers in complete silence and put them under my pillow to dream about the one who would snag my heart.

Jose turned off the radio when I explained that Alma died a few days before Christmas Eve. I asked if he knew anyone in Havana who could check in on and water the forget-me-not seeds that I had planted on *Amistad* street. He promised to ask his cousin to pick some of the flowers to dry and send in a letter to me.

"I went to New York to visit my friend Mrs. Hewson," I said. "She used to be Ms. Harris, but one day a handsome man — who was training to be a diplomat — came into the bank where she worked. Love arose, and soon she became Yolanda Hewson."

We approached the city and turned left to the hills of Reparto Vista Alegre. Jose Saroza honked the horn at a friend and promised to swing by the baseball field after he had dropped me off.

"Mrs. Hewson's husband had many assignments, and they lived in different countries, growing their family — Victor was born in Ghana and Felicity in Cairo. And finally, they came back to New York and moved into the apartment they had left four decades earlier."

"I have also lived in many places — although I have never left Cuba. I want to live here, and I will die here."

"Don't die, Jose," I said, begging. "Not you as well."

"I wish I could go to New York just once — and then I'd tell my children about it every day for as long as I live."

I flipped through the letter that Clara Santos had put in the binder almost a decade before and started reading aloud.

What is time if we do not remember it?

What is life if we do not collect stories for our children and grandchildren?

To save for future generations is to save a little of oneself forever.

Jose held his hands firmly on the steering wheel. Beads of sweat ran down his forehead. He looked out the window, then cleared his throat from the dense silence.

"I'd like to show you somewhere special; shall we say Thursday? I'll pick you up at two o'clock. Don't forget your forget-me-not seeds."

He smiled, like the first time we had exchanged a look to one another in row sixteen. I thanked him for the ride and got off at *Calle 5* — fifth street — in Vista Alegre.

Once again, I stood on ground my feet had never touched before with the backpack next to me. A blue car passed by and honked at the intersection. Hibiscus flowers were in full bloom. Girls in red and white school uniforms ran across the street. A man with yellow suspenders and a cigar in his mouth was selling vegetables from a cart. He sang "Guantanamera" as he made his way down the street. Where was he going?

Time here seemed to move at a half-pace, and the people seemed to get twice as much out of the day — and thus, I wondered, life? It was like in Barcelona, where the day got a few bonus hours when blinds were pulled up and the shops reopened in the late afternoon. Or like the bright sunny evenings of the Swedish summers that patched up the wounds of the dark torments of winter.

Bougainvillea tempted those passing by to come closer to the fences and take in the *art nouveau* style houses from the early 1900s. Dogs barked. It was like time had stalled fifty years ago, and a single day had never ended. The stately iron gate in front of me was the entrance to yet another first meeting. I found the doorbell under a leaf of the grand ivy that was wrapped around the entranceway. It rang when I pressed it, sounding just like the doorbell in Barcelona when I met Rosana Mundi for the first time.

Clara Santos' *"Hola, Felicia!"* was full of anticipation. She kissed me three times in the air when our cheeks met. She wore a floral pattern tank top and necklace with a key on it. The measuring tape around her neck hinted that she had just left the sewing machine to open the door. Another home sweet home — this time with a checkered stone floor in the front hall to cool my warm soles. My feet bore marks of dust, sun, and sandals. The Virgin Mary watched over the pillow in the room I would be sleeping in, directly to the right of the hall, spartanly decorated with a bed, bedside tables, and a wardrobe.

Next to Clara's sewing machine in the living room lay a cherry pink piece of cloth ready for its metamorphosis at the hands of a pair of scissors, a sewing box, a needle cushion, and colorful ribbons. Hundreds of buttons were scattered on a nearby tray next to a yellow rose in a vase.

Clara reached into the rainbow-colored paper bag I had presented her, carefully placing each item on the kitchen table, handling them like a priceless treasure: A bottle of olive oil, soaps with lavender scent, Darjeeling tea, saffron, and a set of five different hand creams.

"I brought them from Europe. I hope you like them."

"I'm the one who must thank you for making the trip here," Clara replied, then she took me by the hand and led me out onto the patio.

We sat down in a pair of rocking chairs in the cool afternoon shade, talking like we had known each other for ages. Coffee sat on the side table. Passing neighbors who I could only see in glimpses through the lush ivy, stopped and greeted us. Clara introduced me as the delightful Swede who had left a binder at a restaurant in Sweden ten years earlier. To the neighbor's surprise, it had traveled the world several times before Clara found it on the bedside table in the guest room.

I went into my room to shower off the dirt and dust from traveling. When I returned to the patio, I was carrying the binder. Clara put her hand to her mouth and began to slowly leaf through it. She stopped when she came to her page, full of memorabilia.

"Look," she whispered. "That's me."

She opened the flap that had held everything in the clear plastic sleeve since 1988. Her gaze rested for a long time on a black-and-white photograph of a ball gown. *For Senator Baron's wife, 1966,* it said on the back. She continued narrating as she looked at the rest of the pictures.

"I sewed this skirt for my mother Rosa García, in the summer of 1974. And look here, the blouse for Señora de la Plata. I wonder what happened to her. It's been so long since I saw her!"

Clara had grown up among artists, who dropped by her family home where the doors were always open. One morning she found a newspaper left on the coffee table with an article about Ernest Hemingway. Clara admired the shirt he was wearing in the picture and set about sewing one just like it. She added an accent by embroidering a sprig of ivy that clung to the shirt sleeve and made a frill around the heart. Clara read her own words — *The Hemingway shirt* — written on the white part of the polaroid before pulling out the last thing left now in the folder. A postcard with ribbed edges.

"Look, Felicia," she said, pointing at the house on the postcard. "This is the only house I've ever lived in. I was born here, and I'll die here."

She turned the postcard over and put on her reading glasses. Her tears landed on her tanned arm, already adorned with a simple pearl ribbon and a constellation of birthmarks.

Memories, like quilts woven from silk-thin yarn, warm us

At night, in the morning

When we are no longer there next to each other

In the cold, in the loneliness

The fragile threads on which memories hang

Naturally fragile

How easily they disappear, in the wind

These gold threads, let me sew the stitches that connect then and now

Now and then

Every now and then

You and me

Forever

* * *

I had closed my eyes while the poem took me places far away and when I opened them again, I was alone on the patio. The empty rocking chair moved rhythmically, but slower and slower. Life took a break, a *siesta* for the senses. In the calm, I found Alma. Or Alma found me. We found each other. She took Clara's place next to me. I remembered the last time I saw her, the morning of December 20th — almost a year ago now — when my bag was packed and ready at the front door where I would soon leave my slippers. Her dining table, the ivy climbing, and the electric

Advent candles. It was snowing outside and had started to freeze. They warned of icy roads on the radio. We hugged and vowed to see each other soon.

The theme of journeys — one from the past and one in the future — were combined in the preludes of Alma's and Nelson's deaths. While Alma and I were overjoyed at the prospect of traveling together, Nelson and Mrs. Hewson returned to his life's beginnings and the long car ride with his father in their last conversation. On his deathbed, Nelson had returned home, and died calmly with his final words, whispered oh so lightly. *I am home, my love. Please come visit.*

It had been written in the stars that Nelson would not wake up the next morning, but not a soul had known that I would never see Alma again after I left her apartment and took the Roslagsbanan train into Stockholm. We were just waiting for the budding spring to burst with joy so we could pack our bags and embark on the journey of our lives in the gallant path of the binder.

Then she died. Gone forever. And I was stuck. Incarcerated, buried alive in a winter darkness that we were supposed to get through together. Together! Not me alone! Alma was no longer alive — a fact of life so strange and difficult to fathom. Sometimes I didn't think about it at all, but then it struck me down suddenly and relentlessly, anytime, anywhere. How I wished I had left her first. She would be better at surviving than me.

Why was *I* the one forced to go to *her* funeral? We had promised each other never to die. Nelson's death was expected. In dark and stark contrast, Alma's passing came with no preparation. Their deaths were on opposite sides of a macabre x-axis, ranging from total awareness to complete oblivion. Which death was worse for those of us left living, if there was such a bloody scale?

My thoughts banged and bounced like a pinball. I was carelessly pulled back and forth, a tug-of-war of the senses. Longing and missing, nostalgia and melancholy, frustration and joy, past and future. Of course, I understood that life and living were the only things that mattered. I could stop living when I was dead.

I remembered being on the swings together, barefoot. Like two pendulums, we swung far, far up in the air, tickled by the sun's rays when our feet touched the rowanberry branches in the summer wind. Memories let me rest in the calm until other emotions took over, and I was forced to move to find new peace elsewhere. I had become a nomad of emotions, always on the run from the dark ground sprinkled with invisible mines under my feet. Deep down, I realized that I couldn't always escape from everything. I needed to deal with the grief; stop and let the darkness take its toll, hold me in its iron grip until it faded into light. It hurt my whole body when I gave in to grief, but eventually the pain cooled, and the aching passed.

Maybe Alma existed anyway, in her own way? And maybe I should realize my dreams anyway, in my own way? Like a day faded into evening, I wanted to rest in for the night and save my energy to power the light of the next sunrise, like a morning glory flower itself. Every new day, a new flower bloomed, a new invitation — a wink — to buzzing bees in search of nectar, the sweetness of life.

My ache for Alma was like a hydrangea, watered by the tearful joy of my memories. Without the tears, its multicolored petals withered. But there were other flowers in my garden. Selma was a shy snowdrop, bursting on the cusp of spring in the muddy mire of my life, still frozen by a winter of grief. Rosana was a sunflower that turned me with her towards the warmth and the light. Mrs. Hewson gave me peace like the scent of lavender, preserved in decorative bags for a dresser drawer. And Clara was the ivy that took root and climbed into my heart.

And I, what was I? Who was I? The blue daisy, or the blue felicia — *Felicia amelloides* — carried my name. First described by my countryman Carl Linnaeus in 1763, as evergreen, upright, blue, and yellow — like my national flag. It was often seen growing in South Africa. One day I would have to go there and pick a bouquet of them.

Throughout my journey, pollen had stuck to the fabric of my mind. I sowed, watered, and harvested in a new garden where life took root again and constantly found new ways to grow. Tears of joy and sorrow eased the drought.

And that's exactly when I heard her voice, loud and clear: *Forget-me-not*, she begged me. *Felicia, Forget-me-not forever.*

* * *

When I regained my senses, I noticed that Clara's rocking chair was empty, but it was still moving a little, slowly. I had been taken over by the painful poison of my grief without any of the usual antidotes I kept at hand: My diary, a pair of running shoes, the TV… Anything that took me away from my real world into another. My gaze stuck on the ivy of the gate and was broken when Clara returned with a wooden chest in her arms. She unbuttoned the necklace and slid the key off its thin chain.

"I've never opened this," she confessed. "I got it from my mother when I was born, in the room where you sleep now."

Clara put the key in the lock and turned it. She took out a package with a silver ribbon that broke when she carefully tried to untie the bow. A light blue cloth bag, so shy in color that it was like ice, had long rested in a cocoon of newsprint from *Rebelde, diario de la juventud Cubana* dated April 26th, 1960. Inside lay a golden garden trowel, about ten inches big.

"L.E.," she said — reading out the letters engraved in a heart of ivy on the handle. "Lourdes Elizalde." And she began telling me a story about true love.

More than two generations ago, a Spanish botanist walked into the bookstore where Clara's great-grandmother Lourdes Elizalde worked. He trod up a path to her heart, and as naturally as that, they fell in love and met as often as they could until his departure. When they said goodbye, it was definite. They never did meet again. When Lourdes Elizalde returned to the bookstore the following day, she found a paper bag on the door handle. In it was a letter and a twig of ivy in a small glass bottle.

Clara reached for the binder that was resting in her lap. She slid her finger across the last rows of a letter written a hundred years earlier by a plant-loving Spaniard madly in love with her great-grandmother.

These gold threads, let me sew the stitches that connect then and now

Now and then

Every now and then

You and me

Forever

"Their invincible love" — she started, pointing to the immense ivy that clung along the wall next to the patio — "manifested itself in a plant that is still growing. Every time I water it, I think of my roots."

The golden garden trowel was passed down one generation at a time. The Spanish botanist never met Clara's grandmother — the baby girl he had fathered. She gave birth to Rosa García, who had Clara at a young age. Four generations of women, still going strong. Clara fell in love and married Osviel, a music teacher in town. One hot summer night, Clara sat in the city's concert hall, blown away by his talent at the Steinway grand piano. When he played "Moonlight Sonata" the music took hold of her with a cosmic force. She experienced something greater than love itself. While receiving a standing ovation, as bouquets of flowers were thrown to him, Osviel blew a kiss to Clara, sitting in a plush chair in the first row. The next morning, he headed out on tour and never came back.

"So, when you called this spring and said that you wanted to come to visit me in Cuba, I instantly knew why the binder had come my way. It was so that I could pass on the greatest ever gardening tool to a woman as dear to me as my own daughter."

And it was exactly what I needed for my solo soul digging.

* * *

At two o'clock the following Thursday, the sound of a moped pulling up and Jose's happy *"Hola buenas!"* could be heard outside the gate. In a sundress and sandals, I jumped on the seat behind the man with the amorous surname Saroza. He was wearing a three-piece suit, hat, and freshly polished shoes.

"We'll be back before it gets dark," he promised Clara, who smiled, obviously reminiscing of youthful days long gone.

"Santiago de Cuba on a moped," she said. "How lucky can one be?"

We sped away in the afternoon heat towards the small church — Basilica del Cobre — that took its name from the copper that had long been mined in the area. Believers made a pilgrimage there and, according to the guidebook, the pope had even once visited. We whizzed through the countryside along a crooked asphalt road lined with villages. My hair blowing in the wind as I held on tightly to Jose's waist, I felt a tingle in my stomach that I wanted to last forever. The emotions that ran through me when I was with

Jose Saroza sailed beyond the sea of romance. It was a rare and endangered animal that would flee and disappear if we tried to capture it.

The contour of the church soon made itself known against the olive-green mountains. Jose parked the moped and opened the massive front door that led into a cool and echoing silence where many souls were present in their human absence. I lit three candles. One for the past. One for the present. One for the future. I closed my eyes and remembered that I had a mission to fulfill for Alma. It kicked off my inner monologue.

> *Dear Ernest Hemingway,*
>
> *It's me again, Felicia. I'm kind of stalking you, I know. This is the third time our paths have crossed.*
>
> *I read in my guidebook that you left your Nobel Prize here in the church in the 1950s? Is it true?*
>
> *You spent time in Gran Hotel La Florida — the mansion in the heights of Barcelona's Tibidabo mountain. Serendipity did not bring me up there. A binder called Amelia did.*
>
> *You dined at La Guarida in Havana, and so did I! One of Alma's last wishes was to go there.*
>
> *Barcelona, Havana, Santiago de Cuba. Three times lucky — it makes me hopeful.*

I was rocked into a cotton-soft elation. When I opened my eyes, I felt connected with the thousands of pilgrims who had visited. Everything was connected from beginning to end. I was the common denominator in my life. My pluses and minuses summed up to the present here and now.

The flow when all is dry

Heading south on Fifth Avenue, I hit the 35 km mark. That's about 21 miles, apparently. I have no idea how long a mile is. I just know the last one is what will get me there. To the end. The last mile.

More than four-fifths done.

The asphalt is like a frying pan and my muscles sizzle like bacon.

So why do I suddenly get such a boost of energy here, on Fifth Avenue?

I've been running nonstop for more than three and a half hours. I turn into a race car, with the gas pedal to the floor, I drive past hundreds of people, but the 40 km sign is nowhere to be seen? Mile 24, mile 25, where are you?

I lose speed. And I know that the slower I run, the longer it will take to finish. And if I quit now, not a single person will come to my rescue.

It's all on me. Everything, right now, is just on me. It always is, but now more than ever.

The more I think about how tough it is, the more frustrating it is that the 40 km marker doesn't appear. Maybe I'm not seeing it because the organizers hadn't bothered to set one up?

I'm so tired it's completely unthinkable to think beyond the next lamppost. Or the next intersection. Or the next traffic light. I count ten steps at a time. One two three four five six seven eight nine ten. One two three four five six seven eight nine ten. And again. One two three four five six seven eight nine ten. And then again. But then there's the scent of autumn leaves. I'm close to the park. Maybe this is the last mile.

My muscles — torched and smoldering — reignite with unimaginable stimulation as I turn right into Central Park, shining in its late autumn wardrobe. The noise level around me gets higher and the street winds its way through, just like the serpentine road in Barcelona that Rosana and I drove along to the mansion on Tibidabo.

I think I am close to the goal, but the road keeps turning. Central Park is taking me for a ride.

Right then, I see it: the 40 km marker. Somewhere in this oasis, I've arrived — like Nelson spotting the rooftop at the end of the long road from Chicago. There's an exuberant joy to know that I'll soon arrive. I'll be home, somehow, in myself anyway.

Now, there's only just over 2 km left. Dear Last Mile, I am all yours for the taking. Please welcome me on your turf.

Ten minutes to go... The equivalent of enjoying an espresso. We all have time. It's just a matter of how we want to dispose of it. A few hours ago, I was far below Manhattan's southernmost point. On a bridge all the way across New York Harbor, where I glimpsed the angular, Tetris-like line of skyscrapers in the sunshine. Now I'm in the city's green lungs, traveling closer and closer to its heart. I have been pumping through its veins since I left Staten Island just under four hours ago.

I've come a long way.

Far from the start, wherever or whatever the start is.

Sometimes a start is a restart.

The end of life, on December 22nd, when my Alma was taken from me. The restart when I decide I want to go on living. I've come a long way. I'm always moving, further and further away from her death, farther and farther away from Staten Island and the western bridgehead of the Verrazano-Narrows Bridge. Closer to a goal. Today, I will defeat grief, and victory will ask my broken heart out on a date.

In that moment of solid joy, I start adoring this test — the human race, the marathon, my life. I marvel at all the memories I've picked up along the way since the starting line: A swirling mocktail of microcosms served as a voyage on foot through all five boroughs — Staten Island, Brooklyn, Queens, the Bronx, and Manhattan — garnished for further sensual pleasure with sounds, smells, and scents of the city. I am neither shaken nor stirred and raise a toast to Alma and sip it.

Kobe, Japan

December 1997

I had been traveling for six months, and time had ticked forward to almost a year without Alma.

We had left the binder at a roadside burger joint at Sweden's north-south halfway point, and, after crisscrossing the globe, it ended up in Japan. Just before Alma's death, Yuzuki Sato — the final person to receive the binder — had put it in a padded envelope and sent it back. Her act of kindness was a treasure map to the forgotten dreams that Alma and I had shared. The last time Alma and I spoke — a phone call that lasted almost two hours — all we could talk about was fulfilling them. But we never imagined that one of us would make this journey alone.

There was so much that didn't turn out as we thought it would on the day that we sent Amelia out into the world along the Edsbyvägen Route 50 in Hälsingland. I had lost my traveling companion, my soul's twin sister. Alone, I had embarked on a trip intended for both of us. I had slept in a bunk bed with Tilda at Anton and Selma's Hämma Manor, gone up into the mountains with Rosana in Barcelona, run a marathon — celebrating the human race — in New York. I had flown on to Cuba, and I met Jose Saroza in row sixteen, then stayed with Clara, who gave me a gold trowel that had been passed down for generations in a house lined with ivy.

Soon one whole year had snuck up on me. How had I stumbled out of bed 365 times without her? I knew deep down that all these questions lining up would be greeted by haphazard guesswork rather than answers. I was tired of thinking. I wanted to pause my brain and refill the tank that had been less than half empty since my life changed paths. My big dream was to become a brighter, complete version of myself. Grab for that famous light at the end of the tunnel.

* * *

The trip from Santiago de Cuba to Osaka — with transits in Havana, Mexico City, and Toronto — finally seemed to be coming to an end when we only had one hour to go until touchdown at Kansai International Airport.

I flipped through a magazine from the seat pocket in front of me. An article titled *Bright Lights in the City* grabbed my attention. It was about *Luminarie*, an annual festival of light in Kobe commemorating the victims of the 1995 Great Hanshin Awaji earthquake.

Every December, an area stretching from Motomachi Station, through the Former Foreign Settlement area to Higashi Yuenchi Park, is awash in lights in memory of those lost in the earthquake. Hundreds of thousands of hand-painted lamps, made with Italian craftsmanship, add to its splendor.

The black-and-white photographs of the aftermath were painful to look at. My pain seemed insubstantial and scattered in contrast to the overwhelming intensity of their torment, which was like a high-density element. I flashed to my physics teacher lecturing about osmium. He explained that it was the best metal for the nibs of fountain pens, like the one he always used to correct our papers, because it was twice as dense as lead. That's how heavy the hearts of Kobe were. I had lost one friend. Kobe had lost six thousand.

Twenty seconds of uncontrollable shaking in the early morning of January 17th, 1995 — measuring 7.3 on the Richter scale — turned Kobe into an inferno. The area west of the city center was completely destroyed. Elevated highways were overturned. Infrastructure toppled. Rubble blocked emergency vehicles coming from surrounding prefectures to help. Many had to dig for survivors with their bare hands, finding nothing or worse than that — death. The lifelines were cut.

The natural disaster had also engulfed the city in flames. Smoke billowed from buildings uncontrollably. Broken gas pipes gave the fires free range to roam. Overnight ferries coming to Kobe harbor reported the smell of gas as they approached the bay. Firefighters stood helpless with their water supply cut. There was no remedy. Lonely, panicked, and desperate survivors were forced out of their demolished homes into the freezing cold. Not everyone who survived the earthquake could live with its aftermath and saw no solution but to take their own lives.

I wanted to play my part in the city's healing. By helping others, I thought — I probably would help myself too. Giving is receiving.

* * *

The captain turned on the *Fasten seatbelts* sign and we went down for landing in the calm black night. I had a perfect view from seat 12A of the sleeping city of Kobe far below me, bedridden between the mountains and the sea. Along the coal-black sea stretched a thin line of light, which garnered strength over the city center and thinned out towards the mountains. A lone radio mast on a peak flashed red in the black, far away from the city. A lost firefly.

I was greeted by an airport decorated with purple orchids and Japanese characters against monotonous backgrounds. Business travelers hurried passed, holding only briefcases. A woman talked on her mobile phone with one hand over her mouth, creating her own little corner in the public space. I made a mental note to call my parents tomorrow.

While waiting for my luggage, I went to a vending machine and used Japanese money for the first time in my life. One one-hundred-yen coin and one five-yen coin got me a bottle of water. I felt the fatigue in my body, and the floor swayed. Comparing the airport clock and my watch — which was still on New York/Cuba time — revealed I had flown thirteen hours into the future. I was undeniably jet-lagged. I took a few quick steps towards my backpack that moved like the conveyor belt sushi I had seen in a documentary about Japanese restaurants. The backpack always came back to me in one piece, albeit a little disheveled — just like anyone else after a long flight. Its new *I love New York* luggage tag reminded me of Victor's stunning eyes. Clara had embroidered FELICIA ÄNG on the side.

I left the baggage hall for a new world — Japan! — where the most important link in the binder's chain was waiting for me. Yuzuki Sato had packed Amelia with care, written Bruno's address on the padded envelope, and sent it back home to Näsby Allé.

*　*　*

I bought a ticket for the high-speed ferry that would take me from Kansai International Airport across Osaka Bay to the east side of Port Island in Kobe. It would dock at a place called K-Cat. How cool a name was that? I had used just about every means of transportation on this trip, and now I was traveling by sea. Kobe, a port city — I liked how the end of my trip was starting to come together.

"Feliiiiiiiiiiciaaaaaaaaaaaaaaa!" shouted Yuzuki when I got off the boat after the half-hour ride. I felt whatever happiness left inside of me try to start dancing.

We drove through the artificial Port Island — built between 1966 and 1981 and inaugurated with the *Portopia '81* exhibition — towards Yuzuki's home in Ojikoen. It was a residential area two stops from the city center on the Hankyu line that was famous for its zoo. The city filled up the entire windshield of Yuzuki's car as we reached the crest of the bridge. Kobe Tower on our left lit up in orange next to a lonely sturdy skyscraper — Yuzuki mentioned it was Hotel Okura and the soft shaped wave-inspired building next to it was Hotel Meriken Park with a passenger ship terminal on its second floor. Kobe stretched left to right, safely guarded by a line of mountains in the back and the sea on the downside. It looked sophisticated, dressed up for a party with its colorful harbor and hotels in undulating shapes next to the sea.

My mind was all over the place. I had landed in the Land of the Rising Sun after a whirlwind voyage through plenty of time zones. Sitting in the passenger seat of a car driven by the friend I'd met for the first time just minutes earlier, I remembered a story from American history:

> *A delegation of Native Americans traveled the hundreds of miles to Washington, D.C., to negotiate a new treaty. The journey was made by train and members of the delegation found the trip to be so fast that upon reaching their destination, they set up their tents to rest so that their souls could catch up with their bodies.*

Now in my sixth destination — following Sweden, Spain, USA, Cuba, and a quick stop in Mexico — countless impressions crammed my mental space. Like those Native Americans, I needed to slow down and catch up with myself, but I also knew that my dark emotions could easily take over in that calm. When the car stopped, I got out and stood once again on a new street in a new city with my old faithful backpack resting against my hip.

* * *

Yuzuki Sato was about the same age as Rosana in Barcelona — in her mid-thirties — and the mother of twins. When Yuzuki was just a young woman studying at Kobe University, she worked at a jazz club called Half Time on the second floor of an apartment building that was a short walk from Sannomiya station, toward the mountains. The sign above the door down on street level read *Established 1978* — a good year indeed to be established — and *Liqur & Snack*. Just like the é missing from the *José* Martí International Airport sign, the o in *liquor* was lost in translation and nowhere to be found.

Half Time seethed with old age. Night after night, its *mama-san* welcomed the regulars who came to drink and play board games. Rumors said the film adaptation of Haruki Murakami's book "Hear the Wind Sing" had been filmed there. Yuzuki had traveled around and even worked in South America after finishing university. She met her husband Reiwa in São Paulo, and when her womb started to swell with pregnancy in the fall of 1994, they moved to Japan. They settled in a cozy two-room apartment above a flower shop along a lively street in the Shinnagata neighborhood west of the city center.

"We were happy, newlyweds, and soon found out I was expecting twins!"

New life was knocking on her door. But then, for a few fateful minutes in the early morning of January 17th, 1995, the earthquake hit. Yuzuki and Reiwa managed to get out of their apartment building, but soon the whole block was on fire.

"We lost my uncle, many friends, and everything we owned… just everything. But we made it. Reiwa and I stayed in an elementary school until it was safe enough to move in with relatives, whose house had not been damaged."

In the wake of grief, Yuzuki gave birth to twins — Rocko and Maya — named after two mountains overlooking

Kobe. They were now almost three years old and curious about the strange new guest who had come to stay with them. I slept in a room with *tatami* mats and a *shoji* paper sliding door. Every night, I took my mattress out of the closet and laid it on the floor. I could plant myself down in soil anywhere on Earth. Grew. Got bigger. Became stronger. But the grief still weighed as heavily and spread like weeds.

* * *

The next day, I walked the short distance from Yuzuki's apartment to her café. It was right on the bustling pedestrian street Suidosuji, which ran through the Ojikoen neighborhood like a lifeline. Its life-loving fishmongers and fruit and vegetable traders brought back memories of Maputo.

There was only enough space for six customers to be in the café at once. Yuzuki served coffee and cheesecake to the tunes of bossa nova. Brazil was the focal point of her love story and the sound of its music teleported her back. Devouring delicious strawberry-flavored cheesecake and espresso, I told her about the Cuban garden trowel in gold that Clara Santos had given me. I had sown forget-me-not seeds in the shade of a palm tree on a slope by the Basilica del Cobre — and poked down some seeds I had smuggled into Japan among the orchids at Kansai International Airport.

"Do you have any good idea where I can plant seeds in Kobe?" I asked, and a lady reading *manga* — wrapped in a textile cover — joined the conversation. She ran a second-hand bookstore close by and asked me to pop by later.

A dogeared magazine from March 1995 featured a double spread photograph of Empress Michiko leaving a small bouquet of narcissuses in a park. The text was all in Japanese.

"The Imperial couple visited Kobe after the earthquake to commemorate the victims," the bookshop owner translated for me, as I stood in her store. "Visiting Shinnagata, an area in west Kobe destroyed in the fires, the empress deviated from the strictly planned protocol, choosing to express herself in her own way with her flowers."

I asked her to write down the name of the park.

"Arigatou gozaimasu," I told her and put the handwritten note of beautiful Japanese characters into my wallet. I made it my mission to find it.

* * *

Pluto the dog started barking when I rang the doorbell later that evening. Rocko and Maya came running. Rocko smiled with a baseball in his hand. Maya wanted to help with all the fruit I had bought on the way. I took off my shoes and followed her.

"Arigatou, Maya." Thank you.

She pulled Yuzuki by the pant leg. Maya reminded me of Tilda with her hair in braids at Hämma Manor, and Alma's little sister Eulalia. A small new generation — a world sisterhood.

Yuzuki prepared juice for the children and opened a beautiful box of Japanese sweets — *nama yatsuhashi* — a gift from her aunt Momoko who had recently visited Kyoto. The triangular-shaped dough was soft with sweet bean paste inside. It paired perfectly with green tea. Momoko-san was a bundle of glee. She was also a widow. Her husband had perished in the earthquake, and the sweet I was holding in my hand took on a new meaning. It was a gift from a survivor — and in that instance, an ocean of gratitude flushed over me. I was grateful that we were both alive, today, here and now.

"You can try some of my peach juice if you want," said Maya, who ran into the kitchen to fetch a glass for me.

"*Arigatou* Maya-*chan, oishi!*" I said. Thank you. Really tasty.

"Now you've got a new friend for life! Maya never shares her peach juice!" her mother called out and laughed.

* * *

The muffled sound of the maroon colored Hankyu trains passing through the nearby railway crossing came at regular intervals. It was Friday night. Maya had fallen asleep on the floor. I thanked my hosts for yet another unforgettable day. Yuzuki started preparing the *ofuro* — the family bath — by first scrubbing it clean. On the display on the wall she set the water temperature to 41 °C, pressed start, and put the cover over the bathtub. Taking turns, the whole family would use the same water. I would go first.

A quarter of an hour later, a melody played from the display, notifying us that the bath was now filled. The bathroom was divided into two sections, with a door in between. I locked the door to the hallway behind me and undressed next to the sink and washing machine. I then opened the door into the shower area. Sitting down on a low wooden stool, I lathered my body with soap, along with shampoo in my hair, and washed it all off using the shower nozzle. Every now and then, I sprayed the mirror clear of its fog and saw myself. Having fully cleaned myself and rinsed off all the foam, I rolled the lid off the bathtub — like rolling cigars in Havana — and put it down on the floor.

I lowered myself into the hot water. Laying completely still, I tuned out everything around me. There was nothing beyond my own being. A moment of zen, with a cool breeze from the window I had opened. Dropping my weapons, I made peace with all my thoughts. Unarmed armistice.

I wrote for a very long time that night. So many thoughts, more than there were words to describe them. So many emotions, which couldn't find the words to fit them. So much of so much. I was overwhelmed. I needed a break.

I wrote about the *Dream of the Seas,* the cruise ship moored at Port Island that we had passed on the way from the airport. Its cabin windows and balconies in long rows had lined the almost endless starboard side along the harbor. Up on deck, travelers had been pointing their cameras to Kobe. Where were they all headed to? I had gotten a taste of boating on my short ride from the airport, but now I dug deeper into the bigger picture. What would it be like to travel from port to port on open water?

My pen moved at lightning speed across my travel journal, leaving a blue ink trace in its path. Tonight, my words provided answers over guesswork. Nighttime daydreaming crystallized a vision in my head. I craved to travel on top of the ocean instead of ten thousand meters up in the air, sailing forward on epic oceans full of time, where there was no hurry. Soon sleep embraced me, and a whole new world opened up behind my closed eyelids.

* * *

I woke up abruptly from a newspaper courier driving past on a moped. It was December 22nd. The anniversary of Alma's death.

I put on a pair of jeans and a sweater and wrote a note explaining that I had gone out. Then I silently closed the door. An elderly man, walking his two dachshunds, nodded at me and smiled. I steered towards the mountains, following a small creek I had seen from my room and heard through the window. A low-pitched boat horn blared far below me.

Without much thought, I continued my ascent upstream. When the road ended, I turned back around, continued downhill, and tried the next street corner instead. Unknowingly, my search for down-to-earth heights in life took me to the Kitano district, where foreign diplomats and merchants settled when Kobe opened its ports to the outside world in the mid-19th century. Preserved European-style mansions gave off a grandeur that grabbed me, a splendor that enticed my sense of sight. They pulled me towards them, like the bougainvillea had tempted passersby in Santiago de Cuba. A white wooden fence tingled my curiosity. What was hidden behind the dense planks?

I followed the plot down a very narrow alley and came to a large gate. A driveway led to a green wooden house with large windows facing the water. An elderly man with a cane came stumbling down the stairs leading to the gate.

"*Ohayo gozaimasu,*" I said haltingly in Japanese.

"*Good morning,*" he replied, as accustomed to English as any *BBC World Service* host. He opened the gate — exposing a new world.

"Hi, my name is Felicia, and I was admiring your beautiful house!"

"My name is Nishida, very nice to meet you."

We shook hands.

"I am going for breakfast where they have the best coffee in town. Why don't you join me?"

"Did you say coffee?"

And just like I had accepted Jose Saroza's ride from the airport because he had a beautiful sounding last name, I said yes to coffee with a stranger four times my age. Nishida-san closed the gate behind him, and off we went. He explained that the house was built for an English couple who moved to Kobe with their three daughters in the 1860s.

"So Felicia, where are you from?"

"Sweden, but I've lived in many places. Buenos Aires, Maputo, Stockholm, Beirut, Paris, and London. I came to Japan from Cuba a few weeks ago. Before that, I was in New York and Barcelona."

"Did you say Buenos Aires? Listen, can you hear it?" he said, stopping mid-step with his index finger to his mouth, motioning me to be quiet and listen. "Can you hear the music?"

For a second, I thought he was a little bonkers, but soon, I could detect the faint sound of a piano in the distance. Tango, the music of my birthplace.

"There is a dance studio around here," he told me. "My wife Anabel and I learned to tango, and as you know — it takes two!"

For a split second, the solo flyer in me felt the pain of the missing piece — Alma — but he soon continued, distracting my thoughts away to worldly matters beyond my own mind.

"I also traveled a lot in my day. My first trip was from here," — he raised his cane and pointed down towards the harbor — "to Brazil. That was almost seventy years ago."

I looked out over the sloping city with streets dipping their toes into the sea. Like Barcelona, Kobe lay warmly wrapped between the mountains and the sea. They were sister cities. Like twins separated at birth and raised in different parts of the world, they both released the same inviting energy that was easy to feel but difficult to put into words. The warm welcome forever ensured that visitors would return.

Nishida-san held open the door to the café inside a house along the quiet pedestrian street high up in Kitano. I was greeted by a setting taken directly from a classic English country home with floral wallpaper, leather armchairs, and display cabinets full of porcelain figures. Portraits on the walls told quiet stories. The owner smiled when we ordered for two instead of Nishida-san's usual solitary breakfast. We each had a thick slice of toast cut diagonally — but not from the corners like the cucumber sandwiches in England — a boiled egg, a mini salad, and a cup of black coffee. Patrons greeted each other joyfully, giving daily check-ins before heading to their designated spots. What better place to sip my coffee than amongst hundreds of years of life stories? Nishida-san treated me to breakfast, and I tried my best to pronounce *Gochisousama deshita* to express my gratitude.

"Now, if you don't mind me stealing a bit more of your time, Felicia," he said, smiling, "I want to show you a place I hold very dear."

The December air was crisp outside. I helped him down the three stone steps, and we walked the winding street arm-in-arm until we turned to the right towards the mountains. With his cane in hand, he made his way one step at a time between deep breaths. We ended up close to the forest at the edge of the city, where heavy tree branches tickled the rooftops. We had arrived at a historical Kobe landmark on a road less traveled. A piece of Nishida-san's personal history. The sign read *Kobe Center for Overseas Migration and Cultural Interaction*.

In the late 19th century, the Brazilian government made Japan a key partner in developing its coffee industry. Brazil needed labor and many Japanese decided to cross oceans for a new life. Facilities were built across Japan to prepare emigrants for the boat ride and life in Brazil. The elongated five-story concrete building — built to evoke feelings of a ship with long corridors and rooms to the sides — became a cultural hub when hundreds of thousands of Japanese emigrated to Brazil in the 1920s and 1930s.

"Let's go inside so I can show you where my memories of life in Japan ended, and our dreams for a life in Brazil took off," he said, opening the door so I could step back into history.

Nishida-san took a moment of silent solace before continuing his story.

* * *

When the cargo and passenger ship *Kasato Maru* left Kobe on her first voyage to Brazil in 1908, many people gathered in the port for a final *sayonara*. Nishida-san's father was a young child and the historic moment left a big impression on him. It aroused a sense of curiosity for places beyond the horizon. The years passed, and when he was twenty-five with enough savings, he was ready to take his wife and son to Brazil in hopes of a better life. He had set his sights on a coffee plantation.

"I was only five years old, but I remember staying here," said Nishida-san as we entered a room, facing the sea, on the second floor. "Me, my Mother, my Father, and some other people slept in here. We learned a little Portuguese like 1, 2, 3, *olá*, and *obrigado*."

Nishida-san pointed to framed black-and-white portraits and group photos where entire families were captured for eternity. A fleeting thought as he spoke — *the missing that stayed ashore, the longing that floated away* — would later be immortalized in my journal. They prepared for what awaited them in Brazil after fifty days on the high seas. The building was on a hill and its roof terrace had an unparalleled view of the city and far over the water. An undertone of moisture reached my nostrils, and the walls breathed history from generations who had wandered on its floors.

In glass cases lay dogeared passports that had crossed oceans decades ago. Portuguese language books and dictionaries were crammed into the shelves. In photographs, people waved white handkerchiefs as the *Kasato Maru* broke free and their loved ones left. Euphoria swept away all uncertainty awaiting them at the Port of Santos.

"I always thought that little boy holding his mom's hand is my father," Nishida-san said, pointing at a picture, his index finger trembling lightly. I reached for his eyes to dry the tears. He took a handkerchief from his coat's inside pocket, and I wondered when he had last cried.

We sat down in pure silence, seizing the moment where our journeys had intersected. Both Nishida-san and I had seen a fair share of the world, and it had brought us exactly here. He described how they woke up in the room upstairs on their last dawn in the Land of the Rising Sun. They stowed away the *futon* mattresses in the cupboards and folded the blankets neatly. Facility staff had lined up at the main gate, bowing as Nishida-san and his family said *sayonara*, following in the footsteps of all the others heading for Brazil. They walked Emigration Road, Iju Zaka, down to the port.

"I held my mother's hand all the way to the sea. Lots of people had gathered along the streets, waving at us! It was like a parade! I remember the excitement still to this day."

It was a sunny summer day in 1929 and for the first time in his life, Nishida-san boarded a ship. They sailed from Kobe on the Indian Ocean via Singapore, around the Cape of Good Hope, and across the Atlantic over to Port of Santos before traveling on land to São Paulo.

They emigrated, like the characters of Karl Oskar and Kristina in the stories of beloved Swedish author Vilhelm Moberg — like my parents, like me. Like so many people who have left everything for a better life. For another life, beyond and without all the guarantees in the world.

I marveled at how I had come across two gentlemen whose lives had been moved by the sea. That massive body of water had played a character in their written and unwritten stories. Ernest Hemingway and Nishida-san. The old men and the sea. Serendipity? I didn't think so. The compass of my life that was lost exactly a year ago today — December 22nd — had pointed me in a new direction. My mourning walk on the anniversary of Alma's death had brought Nishida-san and me together. Without a doubt, he was to inspire the last part of my journey.

For Nishida-san's parents, the few meters in the port became their last steps in Japan. They never returned. A decade after arriving in Port of Santos, Nishida-san's father took over the coffee plantation. Thanks to the agreement between Japan and Brazil, many deliveries went to the port of Kobe, closing the circle. Our morning coffee came from beans grown in the soil of his late father's plantation.

"I have always told my children to sow their own seeds, establish something for themselves," Nishida-san said. "But I also taught them to take care of our family's roots, preserve our past."

* * *

Nishida-san married his high school sweetheart, Anabel, from the Minas Gerais region, and when their three children were in their teens, all five made the trip to Japan. He was eager to show them where his life had begun. Without Kobe, and without that long boat trip, nothing would have happened as it did.

After retiring from the coffee plantation — and passing the business onto his daughter — Nishida-san returned to Japan, bringing his beloved Anabel back with him. They lived happily in Kobe until their days together ran out. Anabel was buried in the Catholic section of the

Nagamine Reien graveyard on the mountainside overlooking the city. She was resting in peace alongside many souls who had crossed oceans in the name of love.

One cold December morning, many years later, Nishida-san went out for breakfast and met me as I admired his house. It was the anniversary of Alma's death. A year without her. I had worried so much, but instead, my journey took a whole new turn that very day. I ripped up my London return ticket and threw it all in the trash.

Kobe, Japan

February 1998

I took the Hankyu train to Sannomiya and changed to the Port Liner, which had been one of the world's first driverless trains when it opened back in 1981. My last train ride in Kobe was on autopilot, my mind running through all the ground I had covered since leaving London eight months earlier. Through the train window, my gaze drifted up and ran along the edge of the mountain that separated Kobe and the sky. My journey with Alma — without Alma — was starting to end. Port Terminal was my stop.

Now a new journey would begin.

My journey.

I got off the train, following other passengers down the escalator and through the electronic gates. Many had started gathering close to the cruise ship. Some would travel, others would stay.

The missing that stayed ashore, the longing that floated away.

In gratitude, I turned around one last time to thank Kobe for life's many events and fates. The past, the present, and the future, all merged into something I could finally understand. It was in the present that I could finally accept my new and future self. I had traveled from London to Leksand and Hämma Manor. From Barcelona, across the Atlantic to New York. Flown to Havana via Mexico City.

Onto Santiago de Cuba and then I'd arrived here in Kobe — by boat.

I had made a new and dear friend: Nishida-san, whose coffee invite had changed the path of my life. I had sunk into *onsen* hot springs of such peaceful calm that I could easily have stayed forever. Nada onsen — not far from Yuzuki's cheesecake café at the end of Suidosoji — had a tattoos-accepted policy. Naturally, it became a hot spring hotspot of the Yakuza. As opposed to most hot springs in Japan, where they were barred, here they could expose their iconic tattoos to the naked eye.

Together with Yuzuki, Reiwa, and the children — Maya and Rocko — I welcomed 1998 by watching Japanese TV shows and eating *toshi koshi soba* on New Year's Eve. Slurping away, they had told me that misfortune and bad luck disappeared when the fragile buckwheat noodles broke, putting everyone on a good path for a long and healthy life.

On January 13th, I got to celebrate *Seijin no hi* — Japan's Coming of Age Day. My twentieth birthday was the next day — January 14th, the name day for Felicia — and I had the honor of wearing Yuzuki's colorful silk *furisode kimono* with sleeves that almost reached down to my ankles. My sophisticated flowery beauty was perfected with white *tabi* socks and *zori* sandals in lacquered wood. I had never felt so graceful — until I started walking! The kimono was wrapped so tight around me my steps only reached about half as long as usual.

My host family had then taken me to Gomoutenjin temple, just up the road from their apartment. Everywhere around me were irresistibly beautiful young women representing the sisterhood — smiling, making victory signs, and taking pictures. I had yet again become part of a big "we." We were one together. We were no longer children. In all our beauty, we would take on a world both infinite and boundless. It was ours to capture.

A few days later, on January 17th, I had joined Yuzuki's aunt Momoko-san in honoring the memory of her husband, who had died in the Kobe earthquake. Survivors had gathered in Earthquake Memorial Park on the west side of Flower Road to light candles for those whose lives were extinguished. Momoko became my friend in grief.

Finally, the day before my departure, I planted forget-me-not seeds in Sugaharasuisen Park, where Empress Michiko left a bouquet of narcissus. My flowers would bloom in the spring, for all those we did not — and never would — forget.

* * *

I gazed at the sea, thinking of the sailing ship *Belle Amie* and all the long-lasting friendship that has taken root in port cities around the world. No wonder it was called friendship. A ship of friends. Each other's ports. Alma's father had mentioned all this to me that cold day in his café — unknowingly setting an ocean motif that I had internalized even before starting this journey. Everything, from start to finish, was connected in one big tidal wave of emotion on which I had somehow buoyed myself. From being completely adrift, I'd come to a place where I could set sail to the future, hopeful.

In the bustling crowd of people, all on their way somewhere, I saw a familiar face. With searching eyes, holding a white handkerchief, and leaning against his cane, he scanned the sea of people. He had walked Emigrant Street all the way down to the sea to say *sayonara*. Tears ran down my cheeks as I rushed towards him. Behind me, I heard a whistle from the deck crew.

"Thank you for inviting me to breakfast when I said good morning outside your gate," I said. The rest of what I wanted to express struggled to come out. "You will forever have a place deep inside my heart. Now I'm going to go and sow my own seeds."

"Your life will bear fruit," Nishida-san said. "Come back one day with your family — you can all stay at my house! Until then, *sayonara*."

I went up the gangplank to board the ship and to start my trip home, by sea and by land. The journey's seeds would eventually turn into lush words, a *life* sentence, the story of my life.

New York City Marathon, 1997

So little left now

Only 800 meters left to go. Half a mile.

Two laps around a running track. Nothing. Now it's almost over, the first marathon of my life. The New York City Marathon. Now I'm almost there.

At Columbus Circle, I know the finish is close.

400 meters to go.

How did I get so far?

How did it happen?

I traveled one step at a time, all the way here. From Alma's grave to the final stretch in Central Park. The starting line was the end. The finish line is the start. I take off my cap and sense a smile inch forward when I suddenly see the finish line.

Finish.

And just like that, it appears right in front of me. After almost four hours of waiting, it comes way too fast. I'm overcome with anxiety — as if the whole thing has been too easy — not difficult enough.

Anyone can do this, right?

I don't want to go on.

I want to keep that feeling of being close but still not there yet.

I cross the finish line with my arms up in the air.

A cry of joy cuts through the sky.

I wake every sleeping angel.

I laugh out loud and cry.

I can do the impossible, and at that very moment, there is only the present.

Here and now, everything is alive.

Always, forever.

Stockholm, Sweden

April 2008

Twelve years had passed since Alma left us. I was thirty years old and heading in a cab to Stockholm Central Station with the aftertaste of stamps in my mouth. What was I getting myself into?

I had left a voicemail and gone off. The flowers for the bridal bouquet would soon sprout in the flower box. All the wedding invitations were in my handbag, and the train was scheduled to depart at 10:06 AM.

I bought a one-way ticket before making a quick stop at Pressbyrån for an orange juice, a *kanelbulle* cinnamon bun, and a paperback book. Stockholm in spring — a beauty on water dressed in budding green — swept by as we pulled out. Putting on a most charming voice, the conductor soon announced on the PA system that coffee was brewing in the café car. I wondered where the beans were from. Brazil? Sweden whizzed by at breakneck speed. Ahead of each stop, he announced on which side of the train the doors would open at the next station.

Several times, I put my newly purchased book in the seatback pocket and walked through the whole train. Through the window in the last carriage, our past disappeared behind us while the future pulled us into it. The present was a constant, the only thing there would ever be. The past was irrevocable, the future was out of our reach.

The last time I had made the trip — in the opposite direction — was in the summer of 1997. I recalled all the station names as we traveled northeast. Uppsala, Sala, Avesta-Krylbo, Hedemora, Säter, Borlänge, Djurås, Gagnef, and Insjön. Tilda had cried in my arms when we said farewell and not until Säter had the tears dried on my dress sleeve.

Selma welcomed me with open arms at the train station at Leksand. It had been eleven years — a moment and a lifetime all at once — since my last visit to Hämma Manor.

"I turned on the heat in the *bagarstugan*," she said. "You'll get some peace and quiet in there, better than staying in the main house."

"Thanks, that's absolutely perfect. Thank you, Selma."

My backpack from when I was a solo traveling nineteen-year-old in the path of Amelia was my trusted companion once again, joined by a cardboard box full of memories. They had been in a safe place for all these years. Soon, the large table that had once been used to make bread was full of letters, postcards, Polaroids, drawings and sketches, photographs, notes, newspaper clippings, train tickets, diaries, drawing pads, maps, and photo albums. The tin box that Alma had bought at the garage sale more than twenty years ago made my heart jump in joy. Just sorting everything in an approximate chronological order took a couple of days.

Around dinner time, I would skip across the lawn to the main house and join Selma, Anton, and Tilda. She was as old as I had been on my last visit. In two months, she would be graduating from high school and taking a gap year volunteering at an orphanage in Ghana. As always at Hämma Manor, the world was immense in its grandeur.

* * *

The Amelia binder lay open in front of me. In one of the transparent plastic sleeves was the letter I wrote to Alma when I was ten years old. It had returned to us in the shipment from Yuzuki in Kobe, just a few days before my first Christmas Eve without Alma in life.

The second plastic sleeve held the two letters Alma and I had written to each other. *Open after I am dead* in solid red marker left no doubts about Alma's instructions. On the back, she had put a heart sticker underneath her name.

"Oh, that's a clear message," I laughed. "Thankfully, you're still alive, so I don't have to open it today!"

"I'm actually really dumb," Alma exclaimed. "What if you die before me?! Did I really think you'd rise from the grave with a letter opener?"

"Well, maybe I should just pack one when I go — just in case! Like the Egyptians, getting ready for the afterlife!"

We broke out in a round of laughter that put us both on the floor.

"So, what about your letter?" Alma asked when we finally calmed back down. "Should I read it?"

"You know what, just wait until the time is right!"

The right time never came. Six months after she died, I did an Amelia Earhart. Solo. It was I, who represented us. I was the one who got to live — and experience — the dream that had been ours. Selma, Rosana, Mrs. Hewson, Clara, and Yuzuki welcomed me into their homes with open hearts. Friends for life, all of them. All thanks to the binder Alma and I left at Jontas Burgers in the summer before I started fourth grade in Paris.

I had kept up with all of them over the years. Rosana had sold her apartment on Plaça de Santa Maria 4 and started life anew in an artist enclave in Òdena, a municipality an hour outside Barcelona. Rosana's pictures of the jagged Montserrat mountain rising out of the countryside tempted me to fly there every time they landed in my inbox. Her mother lived in the area, and her daughter Isabella had always loved to spend time there, so the move had not been that hard. She adapted quickly. Rosana was restoring a farm into a restaurant along a deserted dirt road ten minutes from the highway.

Mrs. Hewson would turn ninety-two this autumn, promising to bring on a party with more champagne than ever. She was still in good spirits, despite recent hip replacement surgery. And she had met somebody. She was in love again.

I had met Yuzuki, Reiwa, Rocko, and Maya in Paris when they traveled around Europe three years ago. The little kids were now teenagers!

Clara Santos was still living at *Calle 5* in Vista Alegre, where she continued to welcome foreign guests in her home. She had started a sewing studio — Clara & Lara — with her best friend for customers who wanted tailored dresses. Of course, it was Clara and Lara who would sew my wedding dress.

And Selma, the life guardian. She'd come to my rescue that morning when I called her.

"Just tell me when you'll be here," she had said. "I'll pick you up at the station."

* * *

The wedding invitations headed for expectant mailboxes postmarked Leksand, April 26th, 2008. We were getting married. The flowers for my bridal bouquet grew and sprouted on the balcony of our apartment in Stockholm. A length of white fabric in Santiago de Cuba was ready for its transformation by Clara & Lara.

The birds were singing. A fly buzzed. I went out on the porch to get some air. The refreshing April spring air shook me a little. I felt alive and looked up into the sky. When I returned inside, I felt Alma looking over my shoulder.

Even as a child, I had always had a dream. It had turned into a promise that I put on paper with my grandfather's old typewriter and slid in an envelope with Alma's name written in my finest handwriting. I was ten years old and the letter went around the world in a binder we had left at a roadside burger stand.

I had opened my letter to Alma when I visited the apartment in Näsby Allé after her death. Since that fateful day in December 1996, I had read my letter countless times. It always made me a little anxious, but something drove me to keep opening and reading it. I had saved it, in the sheer hope that the "helpers" would finally come to my rescue — and so they did — like a marching band with drums and trumpets as I stood barefoot in my nightgown, more tired than usual. The kitchen smelled of coffee.

The cross-breeze of a thought flickered by and the movie started to play again. The idea had visited me countless times before, but today it was like a straight shot to my heart. It was both a relief and incredibly painful. I immediately understood that it was now or never. And never didn't exist. I lost by knockout. No more rounds. Twelve years had gone by.

I let my fingers rest on the keyboard. *ASDF JKL;*

Thumbs on the space bar.

I took a deep breath.

I held down the shift key and typed an uppercase *F*, then *elicia*, space bar, shift key and another *F*, then *anny*, spacebar again, shift key again and an uppercase *Ä*, followed by *ng*.

Felicia Fanny Äng looked pretty written like that.

I hit Enter and started a new paragraph.

For Alma.

I started writing the first chapter.

It was a Tuesday with a scent of coffee. I was more tired than usual, exhausted and completely without energy. The invitations lay in a big pile on the kitchen table. We'd been up all night stuffing and addressing envelopes. Our fingertips were colored gold from stamping Wedding in the upper corners. A morning kiss, with a glass of water in my hand, was the last thing we did. You had to go to a meeting, and I was left standing there, alone in my nightgown, looking at the pile of sealed envelopes. The words we had said to each other still hung in the air.

Stories that had laid dormant for decades sprouted on the blank pages. I finally sowed my own forget-me-not seeds. My memories, for the world to harvest.

Hämma Manor, Sweden

Three months later

Dear Valentina, love of my life

How are you? How are the flowers for the bridal bouquet? Are they blooming?

I've just finished writing the first draft. Does "Forget-me-not Forever" sound like a book you'd want to read? This has been really hard. I've laughed and cried. There are so many letters in the alphabet and words to choose from. It's agony every time I hit the space bar.

Maybe I can collaborate with a flower shop and bundle my book with a bag of forget-me-not seeds?

But I kept an important part out of the story, how you and I met. I thought we'd tell the baby before everyone else. I can feel it move inside, especially when I lie down and rest. I have a feeling it's a girl. Have you thought of any more names?

How many people are coming to our wedding? Have they RSVP'd yet?

I miss you so much. I have never longed for anything as much as I do for you now. I'll be home on Thursday.

I will always love you, no matter what happens. And thank you for letting me write my book. I am eternally grateful to you.

Your Felicia forever

A new email was waiting after dinner.

Hi Felicia,

The flowers for the bridal bouquet are starting to show.

Lots of guests are coming to the wedding!

Oh… the story of how we met! It's been forever since I thought about that family road trip all those years ago. My little brother needed to go to the bathroom, so we pulled over to a random roadside burger place. And there was your binder, waiting for me…

Epilogue

Felicia, Valentina, and their daughter Amica traveled to Japan five years later. They spent a few days in Kobe with "Grandpa Nishida." He was in good health and enjoyed welcoming his new family to his home.

One afternoon, all four walked Emigrant Street all the way down to the sea. In Meriken Park, a short distance from the water, they stopped by a monument that had been erected in 2001 to commemorate all the emigrants who had left for Brazil. *Set sail for hope* depicted a family — a mother, father, and their little son — forever solidified in their leap into the future. With their backs held straight and wearing fine clothes, they were soon to board a ship. A new world awaited them. Standing between his parents, the boy pointed out to the sea.

A new journey would soon begin.

Set sail for hope.

Acknowledgements

A world dream team supported the making of this book and, for that, I am forever grateful. Thank you always.

Maja Svensson and Dave Odegard. Our working relationship started with a letter in the post and a quote by Nathaniel Hawthorne: "Easy reading is damn hard writing." I cannot think of a better way to kick off a partnership. Thank you for guiding me through my own work and for making words such a pleasure to work with. March ahead pancake.

Adele Higgins. I hope to meet you in person one day, so I can thank you from the bottom of my heart. Your invaluable input on the plot, place names, and people made this a better book.

Tomoko Hirasawa. Since my early teens in Barcelona, Japan has been a constant in my life, represented by friendship, travel, and eventually settling here. The relationships I have created are lifelong. We met over coffee and I ran you through my story in Japanese. I am truly honored that you offered to create the cover design, based on your understanding of what the book was about.

Camilla Olsson. Stellar friend who helped me bring the Swedish book to life.

Isak Hjohlman. My cousin Isak offered essential train station advice, taken straight from your experience as a train driver on the route Felicia rides in Sweden. Grateful for insights from a Hälsingland local. *Tack!*

Lena Ryen Laxton. Local knowledge on Leksand was a fantastic addition and helped make this book as authentic as possible in the translation. Tack.

Etsuko Shima Miyamoto. An amazing friend who read the Kobe section and added a facet to its fascinating emigrant history. You are one of my all-time favorites. Thank you ever so much for your support always.

Mohamed Khaled Shawarby. An espresso loving gem of a friend I met in Olympia, you contributed to the Egypt section with valuable feedback. It helped me see my work from an Egyptian who has a truly global mindset.

Maurice Parry. The greatest neighbor ever back in Näsbypark, Sweden, who advised on Marina Läroverket, the school Alma attends in Stocksund. Thanks.

Roberto Sojo. Thank you for great advice on the Spanish phrases I was using. *Muchas gracias!*

Erika Kano Hosoyama. Always on the same wavelength and we truly understand what exploring our surroundings does to us. You nailed it in your message to me: "It is a nice way to befriend and build identity with the place you call home."

Mari Osumi. One of my strongest Barcelona connections, who lived just minutes from me in Tokyo when I first made the move to Japan. Thanks for the support and *azulejos* inspiration! *Moltes gràcies.*

Domenico Italo Composto-Hart: Fellow author who came into my life through a jazz magazine in Tokyo in 2003, and returned in 2020 through our dear friend David Magaña in Barcelona. Thank you from the bottom of my heart for your support and encouragement.

A world of friends who gracefully supported: Hayley Wyatt, Zandra Buud, MaryAnne Jorgensen, Mariela Du Rietz Concha-Ferreira, Chris Wirszyla, Suzanne DeSaix, Carmen Del Campo-Roy, Elisabet Dalseg, Rosanna Benson, Ashleigh Marshall, Belinda Jayne, Pelagia Katsaouni, Liana Acton, Anfisa Kasyanova, Samir Maharram, Nermeen Waheeb, Emery Berger, Agota Szalontai, Louis Santamaria, Nazar Hamdan, Constance Leite Parker, CG Wrangel, Carsten Primdal, Charlotta Wennerström, Agneta Nobel Wennerström, Some kind of relative Lars Andreas Kvick, Susanne O'Leary, Louise Croneborg, Ulrica Robsarve, and Stacy Lorraine. Thank you, in all the languages we speak.

Kerstin Holmberg. Our friendship started my first day of kindergarten and is still going strong.

All my running friends across the world.

Maria and Anders Åsell. My parents, ever supporting from afar this year. *Som alltid, tack till er som till har hjälpt och på har skjutit.*

Charlotta Åsell and Agnes Åsell. The sisterhood. You rock. We rock.

Melvin, Bianca, and Vincent. *Nu köööööööööööööör vi!*

Kazu. Life is good.

Thank you for reading my debut novel
Forget-me-not Forever.

I would love to hear from you, and I promise to write back!

Maybe we can be pen pals?

Instagram @vanessaaselltsuruga

Please visit my website

vanessaaselltsuruga.com

Printed in Great Britain
by Amazon

56938098R00121